Books by the same author

For younger readers
Me and My Big Mouse

For older readers
Dirty Rotten Tricks
They Melted His Brain!
Totally Unsuitable for Children

Jeremy Brown:
Secret Agent

SIMON CHESHIRE

Illustrations by

HUNT EMERSON

WALKER BOOKS
AND SUBSIDIARIES

LONDON • BOSTON • SYDNEY • AUCKLAND

*To our tribe – Robert, Rosemary, Dawn,
George, Isobel, Matt, Susanna, Bob, Jo,
Sophie and all those yet to be*

First published individually as *Jeremy Brown of the
Secret Service* (1997), *Jeremy Brown and the Mummy's Curse* (1998)
and *Jeremy Brown on Mars* (1998) by Walker Books Ltd
87 Vauxhall Walk, London SE11 5HJ

This edition published 2004

2 4 6 8 10 9 7 5 3 1

Text © 1997, 1998 Simon Cheshire
Illustrations © 1997, 1998, 2004 Hunt Emerson

The right of Simon Cheshire to be identified as author
of this work has been asserted by him in accordance with
the Copyright, Designs and Patents Act 1988

This book has been typeset in Plantin

Printed in Great Britain by J.H. Haynes & Co. Ltd

British Library Cataloguing in Publication Data:
a catalogue record for this book
is available from the British Library

ISBN 1-84428-936-2

www.walkerbooks.co.uk

JF

Contents

Jeremy Brown of the Secret Service

Jeremy Brown and the Mummy's Curse

Jeremy Brown on Mars

JEREMY BROWN
OF THE
SECRET SERVICE

Chapter 1

In which Jeremy Brown nearly gets duffed up

··

Jeremy Brown had a secret. His mum didn't know what it was, his dad didn't know what it was, and neither did his younger sisters. Patsy Spudd, his best friend from school, she knew all about it, but she was sworn to secrecy, cross her heart and hope to die.

However, things will get pretty confusing if his secret isn't revealed here and now. Jeremy Brown was an MI7 agent. His boss at MI7 reckoned Jeremy was pretty excellent when it came to foiling evil plots of international proportions. And so did Jeremy. Mind you, his missions were never accomplished easily.

It was a Tuesday, and the weather was grumpy. Jeremy Brown was on his way to school, swinging his bag and watching the clouds grumbling around the sky. He was quite short, quite scruffy, and quite unable to see properly without his glasses, and he didn't notice Sharkface until he walked right slap-bang into him. Jeremy bounced back and landed with a thud on the pavement. Sharkface didn't. Sharkface stayed exactly where he was.

His name wasn't really Sharkface, of course. His name was Mark, but Mark rhymed with shark, and his strange, long nose made his head look sort of wedge-shaped. Even then, people might not have called him Sharkface had it not been for the fact that he was the nastiest bully in the school.

Nervous rays of sunlight crossed Jeremy's face (and his glasses). He couldn't run away, because Sharkface would chase him and duff him up. He couldn't stay where he was, because Sharkface would simply duff him up there and then. Either way, he was going to get his blazer torn. The situation looked hopeless. The situation wasn't really hopeless, as you might guess from the title of this chapter, but Jeremy felt hopeless anyway.

"Brown," said Sharkface, nastily.

Jeremy felt like saying, "What a wonderful memory for names you have, Sharkface," but he didn't. It would only have made Sharkface angry. So instead, he made a sort of whimpering noise, which was more in line with what Sharkface expected.

"I don't like you, Brown. You're a little weed with specs," he said, even more nastily.

"I – I just want to get to school," said Jeremy, as bravely as the situation would allow, which wasn't very bravely at all, to be honest.

"I got an idea," said Sharkface, in the nastiest way possible. If he'd been a cartoon character, a light bulb would have appeared in a think bubble above him. "I'm going to turn you upside down and bounce you on your head." He smiled, and the effect was horrible.

He reached down with both thick, meaty fists, and lifted Jeremy off his feet. He pulled him up close. Jeremy could smell salt and vinegar crisps on Sharkface's breath. He felt something go tight in his throat. Then the same something went tight in his stomach. He braced himself and gritted his teeth.

Suddenly, there was a flash of ginger hair, and the swoosh of a school bag being swung through the air. The bag whopped Sharkface in the stomach, and he dropped Jeremy, who found himself back on the pavement, staring at the sky.

"Oh no, it's Patsy Spudd!" Sharkface moaned.

"What a wonderful memory for names you have, Sharkface," said Patsy.

That made Sharkface angry. He leaped at Patsy with a rumbling grunt. Patsy dodged quickly, and he toppled into a tangle of tree-trunk arms and legs in the gutter.

Patsy stood over him, with her freckle-dotted nose in the air. Or, rather, she stood next to him, since he was at least twice her height, even when he was in a tangle of arms and legs in the gutter.

"Pick on someone your own size," said Patsy loftily. "Come on, Jeremy." She helped him up and they ran.

Sharkface watched them for a moment, with his mouth wriggling into a sneer. It was his way of trying to look tough when he knew perfectly well that he looked silly.

As soon as they were out of his sight, Patsy gave Jeremy a kick on the shin.

"Ow!" yelped Jeremy. "What was that for?"

"Relying on me to rescue you," said Patsy grumpily.

"I keep telling you, I can't blow my cover," whispered Jeremy. "Brilliantly clever and highly trained agents like me must stay in the shadows. I have to pretend to be Sharkface-food at all times."

In his office, the Headmaster was carefully folding an origami elephant. The Headmaster was very round, with a very red face and stubby, sausage-like fingers, but he folded his paper models with great delicacy and skill.

The little finger on each hand pointed outwards as he completed the creature's trunk.

The *bbbbrrrr-ttttrrrr* of the phone made him jump. He twirled in his enormous chair, and the last wisps of grey hair that clung to his head twirled with him.

"Yes! Headmaster!" he barked.

"No, *you're* the Headmaster," said the voice on the phone.

The Headmaster sat up suddenly, and his origami elephant spun to the floor. He'd heard this voice before. His face went a purply shade of mauve.

"Now listen here!" he snapped. "I don't know who you are, but you're not getting me to let Brown and Spudd off school again!"

"Then I presume," said the voice softly, "you don't mind if the whole world finds out that you wear underpants with Frank the Cuddly Bunny on them?"

A purply shade of mauve was no longer good enough. The Headmaster went white.

"H-h-how…? How did you…? I'll have their letters of authorization ready in ten minutes."

To find out whose voice that was, Jeremy and Patsy's history lesson with Mr Plantaganet will have to be interrupted. This won't bother either of them one little bit.

Just as they were busy not paying attention to the details of the Industrial Revolution, Jeremy's left thumb began to tingle. Either he'd accidentally bashed it with a hammer (not very likely in the middle of double History), or he was about to get an important message.

"Sir!" he yelled. "Sir! Got to go to the toilet!"

The rest of the class giggled, except Patsy, who realized what was up.

"Can't it wait, Brown?" said Mr Plantaganet.

"No, sir! Bursting!" Jeremy jigged about a bit in his chair for added effect. Mr Plantaganet waved a weary hand and

Jeremy dashed from the room.

Out in the corridor, he activated the communicator hidden under his left thumbnail. It was a silly place to have hidden it, because pulling out the miniature aerial always hurt.

"Ooo, ow!"

The earpiece was concealed under his right thumbnail. He spoke into his left thumb, with his right thumb jabbed into his ear. He put on a very serious expression and gave his identification code: "MI7, the custard is banana flavoured."

"With fruit portions," said the voice. "Pay attention. This is Control. Three days ago, the Com-Star communications satellite developed a fault and dropped out of orbit. It will crash somewhere in your sector in approximately fifteen minutes. It's designed to withstand impact, so it should land in one piece. It's roughly the size and shape of a dustbin. Your mission is to retrieve it, before anyone else does."

"Anyone else?" muttered Jeremy, slightly worried.

"It contains experimental computers which are years ahead of their time, stuff that any of the world's worst villains would pay millions for."

The bell rang, doors opened, and the corridor was suddenly filled with the sounds of clattering feet and chattering voices. Patsy appeared as Jeremy quickly pushed the miniature aerial back into place.

"Ooo, ow!"

"Are we off?" said Patsy excitedly.

"We're off," said Jeremy. And off they went.

As they left the building, the Headmaster came running up to them, puffing and panting. Trembling, he gave them each a letter of permission to be out of school. He had a helpless grin on his face, and kept dabbing a hanky to his forehead.

"Here you are. Er, have a nice time," he said, and quickly wobbled back to his office.

"You don't suppose he suspects?" whispered Patsy.

"No, he doesn't suspect," said Jeremy, with a grin.

They hurried to the school gates, and Jeremy told her about the message from HQ.

"How can they be sure it's going to fall somewhere around here?" said Patsy.

"Well, er, they'll have followed its trajectory … thingummy. Or something," said Jeremy, who paid even less attention in Maths than he did in History.

Now it was time to set off on another daring, dangerous, deadly and other-things-beginning-with-"d" mission, it was also time for Jeremy to smarten himself up. Being quite short, quite scruffy and quite unable to see without his glasses was just a disguise. Suddenly he stood up straight, did up his shoelaces, and popped his glasses into his top pocket.

"At last," he said with a sigh, pulling up his tie properly and making his eyes go all narrow and tough-looking.

"I do so hate having to look scruffy."

Patsy, on the other hand, was quite happy to be her normal self, ketchup-stained and looking like she'd been dragged through a hedge backwards.

"Come on," she said. "We haven't got long."

Chapter 2

In which an evil scheme is hatched, and a satellite drops to Earth

....

Meanwhile, on the other side of town, in an abandoned factory, deep in the remains of a damp and musty basement, three of the country's most notorious and despicable villains were practising their French.

"Vooz ett ern ... cosh-on trez gross," said Kenneth. He was almost two and a half metres tall, with shoulders like a couple of medium-sized sheep fighting under a blanket, and a face like a bulldog that's been chewing a wasp. As he read the words, he followed them on the page with a grubby thumb. "You are a very fat pig."

"Vooz ett ern cosh-on trez gross," repeated his brother, who looked exactly the same and, by a strange twist of fate, was also called

Kenneth. Their mum had been a terribly confused woman.

Neither of them was worried that their pronunciation was terrible. They were reading an article entitled "How to Insult People in Thirteen Languages", which appeared in the new issue of *Thug!*, the club magazine of ROTTEN (the Rancid Organization for Terror, Threats, Evil and Nastiness).

The third villain, a tall and wiry man with a tall and wiry moustache, stepped out of the shadows. His name was Sid Lime, and his eyes appeared to have been borrowed from one of those paintings which follow you around the room in creepy old houses. "Amateurs," he spat with a growl.

"We're expund— expind— we're biggering our education," said Kenneth and Kenneth together. First-Kenneth scratched his head, and Second-Kenneth scratched his bottom.

"Listen," hissed Sid quietly. He didn't need to hiss quietly, because there was nobody for miles around, but he reckoned it was a more villainous thing to do. "Listen, you micro-brained dollops of chimp poo. While you've been eating extra bananas to get enough skins to slip under the feet of old ladies, some of us have been doing serious research."

With a flourish of paper, he flicked open his copy of *Wrong Doer*, the newsletter of SCUM. (SCUM was the Society of Criminals; the U and the M didn't stand for anything, but SC didn't sound like much on its own.)

"There! Read the headline!"

First-Kenneth mouthed the words carefully. " 'I Lied, Confesses Frankenstein – Monster Was Man in Suit!' "

"No, above that," said Sid.

" 'Five Minutes to Go Until Satellite Hits Town – Dash for Computer Secrets Is On!' "

Sid folded the newspaper with a couple of lightning movements and stuffed it into his pocket. "By the end of the day, gentlemen, we will be richer than a millionaire in a thick chocolate sauce. Move out!"

Sid marched towards the stairs, cackling in the high-pitched manner approved by the official SCUM handbook. Kenneth and Kenneth followed, giggling excitedly.

Sid's voice echoed around the dripping, shadowy walls. "Hurry, gentlemen. I estimate that the satellite will appear in the sky any second now!"

"Patsy, I estimate that the satellite will appear in the sky any second now," said Jeremy, peering through his binoculars and tapping his pocket calculator. They were standing on the corner of the high street, getting funny looks from shoppers.

"Whereabouts?" said Patsy, looking up and leaning back as far as she dared.

"Umm, up there somewhere, definitely." He tapped at his pocket calculator a bit more.

"I'd say," said Patsy thoughtfully, "that it'll appear as a small red streak of flame, visible on a direct line from this spot past the roof of the greengrocer's."

Jeremy stopped tapping and looked at her, eyes wide. "That's a remarkably precise and confident prediction," he said. "How can you know that?"

"Because there's a small red streak of flame visible on a direct line from this spot past the roof of the greengrocer's."

Jeremy whirled around and looked at the red streak through the binoculars for a moment. "Now, judging from the angle of descent (*tap – tap – tap – tap*) and the speed of motion (*tap – tap – tap – tap*), and all that kind of stuff, we can calculate that it will land in (*tap*), crumbs, Brazil!"

Patsy snatched the calculator from him. "Oh, give it here." She did her own sums. "It's coming down somewhere near the sewage works," she mumbled.

"Oh, *yuk!*" cried Jeremy. "I'll get *filthy!*"

Patsy consulted her fold-out map of the town. "Ah, no, not the sewage works…"

"Thank goodness for that."

"It's going to land on the school."

"WHAT?!"

"Exactly!" cried Patsy, flipping her hair out of her eyes. "It'll have to be evacuated!"

"No," said Jeremy, "I mean, 'What? We've got to go all the way back there again?' It's miles. Did I ever tell you about the time I was blasted 476 kilometres into space by a pair of exploding underpants?"

"Many times," said Patsy wearily.

They set off for the school. Jeremy hoped that, whatever happened, they didn't come face to face with a gang of desperate, greedy criminals.

Meanwhile, the gang of desperate, greedy criminals had got a head start on them. Sid, Kenneth and Kenneth were sitting outside the school gates in Sid's huge, black car. Sid was keeping a beady eye out for trouble. Kenneth and Kenneth just had beady eyes.

Sid glanced up at the sky and caught sight of the red streak, then he glanced at the school gates and caught sight of Jeremy and

Patsy hurrying towards the main buildings. His brain put two and two together, made three, and added one.

"They know what's going to happen," he hissed quietly (which was probably the right thing to do this time, since our heroes might possibly have overheard him). "They must be working for the cops, or MI7, or something else disgustingly well behaved."

The red streak was getting brighter now, and larger every second. Jeremy and Patsy could hear a high-pitched whine, getting steadily louder.

"What do we do about them, boss?" said First-Kenneth.

"Bet he says to get 'em," whispered Second-Kenneth.

"Do, gentlemen? We GET THEM!" shouted Sid. He slammed his foot down on the accelerator, and the car's wheels squealed as they spun into action. The car leaped forwards, heading straight for Jeremy and Patsy.

"Told yer," said Second-Kenneth with a grin, clapping his hands in glee.

The car bounded past the gates at top speed. Its engine roared.

"That satellite sounds ever so near," said Jeremy, looking the other way.

Patsy spun on her heels. The car was almost upon them! No place to run! She leaped sideways, knocking Jeremy off his feet. The car screeched past, tyres missing them by millimetres. Sid hissed with anger.

"Are we going back to get them again?" said Second-Kenneth.

"No, pea-head, we're going to get to that satellite before they do!" spat Sid. The car shot on towards the school buildings.

All that blocked their way was Sharkface.

The red streak had become a flaming column of smoke. It whistled as it plummeted through the air, closer, closer.

"Of all the rotten luck," said Jeremy, dusting grass off his trousers. "A gang of desperate, greedy criminals."

Suddenly, the satellite came screaming out of the clouds, and walloped smack through the roof of the school with a sound which can't really be put into a word but which was more or less *WHHHhhhAAAAaaammmmM*!! An explosion of dust, debris and sections of roof puffed out into the sky.

"Quick!" yelled Jeremy, standing at a slight angle, trying to look heroic. "Those villains mustn't get to it first."

Patsy's hands were pressed to the side of her head. Luckily, what she said next turned out to be completely untrue, so there's no need to worry: "I bet it's gone through about three floors. I bet there are loads of injuries and blood all over the place."

Sharkface stood in the way of Sid's car, hands on hips, sneer on face. He wasn't being brave, just plain stupid. Sid put his foot down. Sharkface tried to jump, too late. Next thing he knew, he was clinging to the car's bonnet, one hand on each headlight. The car smashed through the doors of the main building, scattering teachers and splinters of wood.

"Aaaarrrggghhhh!" screamed Sharkface.

The sound of the car was deafening in the corridor. Its wheels spun, and it lurched forwards, then turned a sharp left and bump-bump-bumped up the stairs.

"It's up here, and I want it!" said Sid.

"Aaaarrrggghhhh!" screamed Sharkface.

Jeremy flapped his arms to clear the smoke in the corridor. Patsy picked up a chunk of door, ready for a fight.

"There's no need for that," said Jeremy. "All we need is a brilliant idea to get us up a couple of floors before their car can smash its way there."

"Such as...?" said Patsy.

Kids were rapidly collecting in the corridor, their jaws hanging lower than a snake's kneecaps.

"The Chemistry lab!" said Jeremy.

"But we're both terrible at Chemistry," said Patsy. "Everything we touch explodes."

"Exactly!" Jeremy dragged a desk out of the lab, into the corridor, and put another on top of it. Then he collected a large beaker and an armful of dangerous-looking substances. "Get in between the desks," he said. He mixed all the chemicals in the beaker, and jumped in beside Patsy.

With an almighty *WHUMPH!* the mixture ignited. It was a result which would have scored Jeremy zero in an exam, but which shot two desks, one secret agent and one secret agent's best friend, through the ceiling, through another ceiling, and landed them in the Headmaster's office.

"There you are," coughed Jeremy through a cloud of dust. "Am I a genius or what?"

The car revved up another flight of stairs. Sid spun the steering wheel, and the car ploughed through a bookcase. Mr Plantaganet had been looking forward to an afternoon reading his new textbook entitled *Crop Rotation Methods in Fourteenth-Century England*. He realized that he'd probably have to miss out on that particular pleasure today, since he now found himself jumping out of a hole in the wall and into the school swimming pool.

First-Kenneth pointed a stubby finger at the kid clutching on to the bonnet of the car. "Hey, his head looks like a shark."

The car took the corner off a classroom, and a shower of plaster and falling bricks jerked it to a halt. Sharkface flew off the bonnet, out through an open window and joined Mr Plantaganet for a swim.

Sid, Kenneth and Kenneth climbed out of the vehicle.

"Spread out, boys," said Sid, coughing as the dust settled. "It's around here somewhere."

And so it was. Nearby, in the Headmaster's office, Jeremy and Patsy realized where they were, and prepared their apologies. Then they saw a large, scorched, cylindrical object, steaming gently and sitting in the spot usually occupied by the Headmaster.

"I hope that's not him," said Jeremy.

It wasn't. The Headmaster was underneath the large, scorched, cylindrical object, pinned to the floor. Origami animals were scattered all over the place. Luckily for the rest of the school, the Headmaster's stomach had broken the satellite's fall. He groaned painfully.

Jeremy and Patsy peeped over the edge of his desk and waved tiny little waves at him. They had sheepish smiles on their faces.

"Hi, sir," said Patsy. "Give us a minute, and we'll have this out of your way."

The Headmaster's face went the red it usually reserved for major breaches of school discipline, or parents' evenings. "Kfluff mnnemm flumm ploo!" he spluttered.

"He's gone barmy," said Patsy, fearfully. "Look, he's frothing at the mouth."

"No, I think he's just swallowed half a dozen origami animals," said Jeremy.

"Or perhaps," said a sinister voice behind them, "he's realized that the game is up."

Jeremy and Patsy spun around. Of all the things that could have happened at that point, the best would have been for Jeremy, having secretly picked up a handful of plaster dust, to fling it at the villains. They would have coughed and rubbed their eyes, allowing Jeremy and Patsy time to escape with the satellite, identify the villains to MI7, and get them picked up by the police.

Unfortunately, all Jeremy could fling was a giraffe made out of a page from an exercise book. It bounced off Second-Kenneth's nose.

"Oh, rabbits," said Patsy. "I suppose that means we're going to be captured and locked up in a dark, stinking basement in the middle of nowhere."

Chapter 3

In which our heroes are locked up in a dark, stinking basement in the middle of nowhere

....

"You just had to say it, didn't you?" grumbled Jeremy. Patsy poked her tongue out at him.

The basement was even damper and mustier than it had been on page 24, and Sid, Kenneth and Kenneth being there only made things worse. Grey-green mould grew in hideous lumps across one wall. The smell of week-old cabbage hung in the air. A bottle of Super-Strong-Ultra-Germkill Detergent would have taken one look at the grime on the floor tiles and had a screaming fit. The only light came from a tiny, smeary window, way up high above them. Jeremy and Patsy were sitting (carefully) on an upturned crate. Their left legs were chained to one of the many pipes which snaked around the walls.

Jeremy wriggled, a sour expression on his face. "I'm getting my best trousers all grubby now. And we've missed lunch."

Patsy was about to say, "Stop thinking of your stomach for once and start thinking up brilliant ideas for getting us out of this dangerous and terrifying situation!" but was interrupted by the sound of the news on the portable telly Kenneth and Kenneth were watching in the far corner. They weren't really interested in the news, they were waiting for the cartoons to come on.

"—which fell to Earth earlier today, landed safely on the stomach of Grotside School's headmaster," said the tinny voice from the telly. "The disturbance at the school was witnessed by teacher Brian Plantaganet."

"Brian," sniggered Patsy quietly.

Mr Plantaganet appeared on the screen, dabbing his face with a towel. "There were dozens of them," he said, trembling. "They drove through school in eight bulldozers! I blocked their way as best I could, but after a long fight I was hurled through the roof. Savages, that's what they were! Maniacs!"

The newsreader came back on screen. "By the time the police arrived in a fleet of blue vans, the criminals and the satellite were long gone—"

Sid stabbed the "off" button. For a moment, the only sound was the dripping of a particularly nasty and germ-filled goo from the high ceiling. Then came the slow *K-clack K-clack* of Sid's boots as he walked over to his prisoners. Behind him, Kenneth and Kenneth quietly found a spare tape and set the video for the cartoons.

Jeremy, being a highly trained secret agent, faced Sid with a bold and steadfast expression on his face, his back straight, his mouth set in a slight sneer. Patsy, however, not being a secret agent, let her bottom lip wobble uncontrollably.

K-clack K-clack K-clack.

Sid had been on the phone for the past hour. He'd worked his way through the

Baddies (International) section of Yellow Pages, and had found the phone number of the most unpleasant and disreputable computer thief in the world. The thief had been on the loo when Sid phoned, but his mum had got him to call back, and they'd settled on a price for the satellite. After he'd put the phone down, Sid had consulted his SCUM handbook, which had informed him that he should now approach his prisoners slowly, wearing noisy footwear, and say:

"Allow me to introduce myself. I am Sid Lime." The low, sinister sound of his voice bounced off the walls, found it had picked up something nasty from them, and died away.

"Good afternoon," said Jeremy politely. "I am Jeremy Brown of the Secret Service, and this is my sidekick, Patsy." Patsy kicked his side. "Sorry, this is my Executive Assistant, Patsy."

Sid gave a high-pitched cackle, as recommended in the SCUM handbook.

"Secret Service? Hah! Do they seriously believe that mere kiddies are going to stop me? I've just been on the phone to the most unpleasant and disreputable computer thief in the world, and very soon I and my colleagues here are going to be so rich they'll have to invent a new word for greedy." He gave an even higher-pitched cackle.

"They'll certainly have to invent a new word for ugly," said Jeremy.

Kenneth and Kenneth giggled, then realized he was talking about them too, and kept quiet. Sid leaned close to Jeremy, his yellowy teeth showing through a broad grin. Jeremy could smell cheese and onion crisps this time.

"My colleagues and I are now off to the rendez-vous point. By the time anyone finds you – *if* anyone finds you, that is – we'll be thousands of miles away. Come, gentlemen, we have an appointment in three hours' time. Fetch the satellite and meet me by what's left of the car."

He ushered them out, pausing only to give Jeremy and Patsy a cheery wave. If his cackle had been any higher, it would have missed his face completely. The door slammed and locked behind him with a heavy *claaanng*.

Then there was only the dripping of ooze from the ceiling.

"Oh dear," said Jeremy quietly.

Patsy kicked her leg about, making the chain rattle wildly. "Jeremy, old pal, now would be a good time to tell me that you've got a special chain-cutting type device hidden in your shoe, or a laser gun in a biro or something."

Jeremy raised an eyebrow. "Let's not be silly, Patsy."

"Can't you get MI7 on your radio?"

"We're in a basement, remember?" said Jeremy with a sigh. "That window way up there is at ground level. The signal won't reach them."

Patsy rattled her chain again, angrily. Rattling it made her feel better, so she rattled it some more. Meanwhile, Jeremy paced up and down as far as his own chain would allow. Wrapping a hanky around his hand to avoid contamination, he tapped gently at the pipework to which the other ends of their chains were attached.

"I wonder what's in these pipes?" he said, almost to himself. "If it's gas, or oil, we'll be in real trouble. Again. But if it's water…"

Patsy's freckled nose wrinkled excitedly. She could smell an escape plan taking shape, and escape plans usually meant a certain amount of noise, violence and damage to property. "What do you want me to break, J.B.?" she said, pulling up her socks and wiping her nose.

"These pipes," said Jeremy. "We'll both get dreadfully wet, of course, but that's unavoidable. *If* the pipes carry water."

Patsy's leg swung back, ready to give the pipe an almighty whack. "And if it's oil?"

"We'll come to a sticky end."

"And if it's gas?"

"We'll get blown to bits."

Patsy stuck out her bottom lip and nodded thoughtfully. "Right, better give it a really good boot, then."

She kicked the pipe. It wobbled and clanked against the wall. Another kick. It bent with a screech of metal. Another. The bend became a dent. Another. The dent became a buckle. Another. The pipe cracked and snapped in two. The chains spun free.

Jeremy and Patsy's relief that it was water which shot out was rather dampened by the fact that the water was absolutely freezing. It gushed and rushed across the basement floor, soaking everything. As it hit them, they let out howls that would have got a werewolf through to the national finals of the All England Howling Championships.

"Ha–haaaa! Who's for a swim?" yelled Patsy, a broad grin across her face. Jeremy's teeth were chattering too much for him to answer.

*　　　*　　　*

It took quite a while for the whole basement to fill with water, so we'll skip to the bit where Jeremy and Patsy were floating level with the window. The broken pipe was way below them, gushing silently now in the murky depths of the room.

Patsy swam over to the window with a powerful front crawl. She grabbed the frame with both hands.

"You'll have to give it a good pull, I expect," spluttered Jeremy, trying hard to keep afloat. Underwater, his arms and legs were doing a rapid doggy-paddle. "Judging from the terrible pong in this room, it hasn't been opened for years."

Patsy summoned up all her strength, then sent out for a double side order of extra, just to make sure. The water rose higher, splashing the grime-streaked pane of glass. She breathed deeply, and gripped tighter. She pulled.

Nothing.

She pushed.

Nothing.

"It won't budge!" she shrieked.

The water continued rising. There was just enough room between it and the ceiling for their heads and shoulders now.

"Try again!" called Jeremy. "The window frame's bound to be rotten through."

She gripped hard and pulled, and pushed, her face stretched tight with effort. Nothing.

"Nothing!" she yelped.

Patsy looked at Jeremy, and Jeremy looked at the window. So much for his escape plan.

"Hang on a mo," he said suddenly. He tried to doggy-paddle over to the window, but the strength of the water currents pulled him back into the centre of the room. He tried to shout to Patsy, but kept bobbing under the surface. All he could do was make a turning motion with his hands.

"Huh?" said Patsy, frowning. She was having trouble keeping afloat herself. The water was fast approaching the ceiling, and the muck on the ceiling was making the water wish it had never left the pipe in the first place.

Then Patsy realized what Jeremy meant. She felt along the window frame, found a tiny little catch, and flipped it open.

Water gushed out into the open air, and the two of them gushed along with it.

They were in a scruffy, weed-covered and now soaking wet courtyard. They staggered to their feet, coughing and trying to ignore the horrible smells that were clinging to their clothes. Patsy gave a thumbs-up sign. "That was fun!" she said breathlessly.

Jeremy tried to smooth his hair back into place, and actually did quite a good job of it. "I really am quite frighteningly clever," he said. "Did I ever tell you about the time I escaped from a pit of poisonous snakes using only a rubber band, a silk handkerchief and a positive attitude?"

"Yes," said Patsy. "Call MI7, quick. The satellite could be anywhere by now."

Jeremy pulled out the hidden aerial of his communicator. "Ooo, ow!" He shook both thumbs a couple of times. "No good, it's completely waterlogged. We're on our own."

Patsy shook herself like a dog. "Oh, rabbits. There must be some way of knowing where they've gone. The ratty little one said they had a meeting in three hours. He also said they'd be thousands of miles away soon."

They stood and thought carefully for a moment.

Chapter 4

In which our heroes have worked out that the answer is the airport

....

"Your attention, please." A crisp, female voice echoed around the polished halls and corridors of Terminal One. "This is an important announcement. Will all passengers tronpolling on the glumpy plinky plonky, make sure that flumpy dinky doo, bim bom pilly clump. Thank you." The airport announcer had no idea why they made her say such things. It's a well-known fact that airport announcements sound like gobbledegook. Less well known is the fact that they *are*.

Jeremy and Patsy had put on dark glasses in an effort to look more official and dangerous. Their clothes were crumpled and damp, so the effort was completely wasted, but they reckoned they looked pretty cool in shades, so they kept them on.

"We must try to blend in and be as inconspicuous as possible," whispered Jeremy. He straightened his tie, which was now all twisted and curly, and they looked around at the shifting crowds of passengers and the blinking display screens.

"I can't see the blinking display screens 'cos of these blinking glasses," mumbled Patsy.

"Whassall this then?" said a low voice beside Jeremy's right ear. Jeremy almost jumped out of his skin, but didn't, thanks to his knowledge of the MI7 leaflet, "How Not to Jump Out of Your Skin". They turned, to find a dozen security guards looming over them, with their long truncheons and short tempers at the ready.

"You are herewith looking of a highly suspicious and non-passenger-style nature," said another guard.

"My name is Jeremy Brown," said Jeremy correctly, "and this is my – Operations

Director, Patsy Spudd. Glad to see you chaps are on the ball. Now, if you'll run along, we're on official business of a highly sensitive and non-airport-style nature."

The guard with the narrowest eyes and the widest nose leaned closer. He sniffed Jeremy, and his eyes suddenly widened in disgust. "If you're on official business, sonny Jim, then I'm the Queen of Sheba."

"We'd love to stay and chat, Your Majesty, really we would," said Jeremy, "but we've got important work to do, catching a gang of international computer thieves."

Unfortunately, if there was one thing the security guards wouldn't stand for, it was someone else doing the chasing of villains in their airport. All together, they snatched pairs of handcuffs from their belts and flipped them open. "You're coming with us!" they all bellowed.

Fortunately, if there was one thing that Jeremy Brown was famed for at MI7, it was having amazing pieces of good luck at moments like this. The amazing piece of good luck he had at this particular moment involved a large crowd of Japanese tourists sweeping past, allowing him and Patsy to conceal themselves among the luggage and souvenir hats. By the time the guards had stopped answering questions about where to find the check-in desks and the toilets, Jeremy and Patsy had long gone.

They sneaked away from the crowd just in time to avoid being put on a non-stop overnight flight to Okinawa. (Patsy had made several friends, and swapped addresses and photos with a Mr and Mrs Kawamishi from Tokyo.) They headed off towards the departure lounge.

"Keep a look-out for a large rucksack," said Jeremy, "or something else large and travel-related that they might have stashed the satellite in. Even that lot aren't so stupid as to carry millions of pounds' worth of stolen high technology on open view through a public place."

*　　*　　*

First-Kenneth was dragging millions of pounds' worth of stolen high technology across the floor towards the check-in desks. He was struggling because it weighed almost three tonnes, and because heat-scarred bits of its outer casing kept getting caught on the carpet. Second-Kenneth was too busy hitching up his trousers to help. It was Second-Kenneth's belt that his brother was using as a rope with which to drag the satellite.

Sid had gone to the third phone booth from the left, next to the queue for Flight DH103 to Spain, as he had been instructed. He had dialled the number he'd been told to memorize, and had now been informed by the most unpleasant and disreputable computer thief in the world's mum exactly where the plane would be waiting for them.

He returned to Kenneth and Kenneth.

"Gentlemen," he said quietly, his eyes

darting in all directions to make sure nobody was sneaking up on them.

"Can you see all right with your eyes like that, boss?" said Second-Kenneth.

"Shut up. Everything is arranged. We now go to the departure lounge and wait for a contact to contact us. We will board the private jet of the most unpleasant and disreputable computer thief in the world, we will be given a quite disgustingly large sum of money, and then his mum says it's OK to get a lift to Brazil. Oh, and we're to make sure he's wearing his woolly jumper. He got wet today, apparently, and he might have caught a chill."

They arrived at the departure lounge in the space of one short sentence. The satellite bumped along behind First-Kenneth, leaving a trail of little bits of metal behind it. Second-Kenneth scampered off to the shops to get some comics and dolly mixture for the journey, and Sid found somewhere to sit away from the law-abiding folk.

Jeremy and Patsy, crawling along on their hands and knees to keep out of sight of the gang, were soon positioned underneath Sid's chair. The alert reader will have already worked out how our heroes had tracked the gang down. Any readers who are not alert have jolly well missed out now.

"Lucky you told them this gizmo was a shaving kit," dribbled Second-Kenneth through a mouthful of liquorice (the shop had sold out of dolly mixtures), "or we might not have got it through customs."

"If we bring their buyer to justice," whispered Jeremy, "we could deal a deadly blow to world computer crime."

"Or at least give it a good poke in the eye," whispered Patsy.

"I'd be famous!" whispered Jeremy.

"No, I'd be famous. You're a secret agent."

"Oh yeah."

They didn't have long to wait. A figure wearing a long, dark raincoat, black gloves and a wide-brimmed hat to keep his face in shadow, walked briskly past. He looked every inch the despicable low-life, and Sid was dead jealous.

"This way," said the figure, a hanky held to his mouth to disguise his voice. Jeremy only caught a brief glimpse of him, but noticed that there was definitely something shark-shaped about his head.

Sid jumped up. From their hiding place, Jeremy and Patsy saw a sudden confusion of three pairs of feet.

"Come along, gentlemen. Careful with the merchandise. Oh, for heaven's sake leave the sweeties, you can get some more later."

The feet hurried away, followed by the heavy dragging sound of the satellite.

"Red alert, Patsy!"

They scrambled out and followed, hurrying from doorway to waste bin, waste bin to behind-the-corner, behind-the-corner to behind-somebody's newspaper. The gang were led out of the terminal building, and on to the vast, open stretch of concrete which led, in turn, to the airport's runways.

From around the corner of the terminal building came an unmarked aeroplane, its jet engines shrieking, ready for take-off. It was much smaller than those used to take tourists on holiday. Jeremy, concealed by a security patrol car, estimated it would seat about two dozen people.

"So with Fatty and Fatty II: The Sequel, it'll be quite a squash," yelled Patsy above the din.

The plane taxied slowly in a wide circle. The howling of the engines rose and fell as it manoeuvred. The mysterious figure stepped forward, holding his hat on to his head, and beckoned to the gang. A door in the side of the plane swung open, and a short stepladder dropped out. It was soon fixed, and the villains boarded the plane. At least, two of them boarded the plane, the other two sort of squeezed in painfully, grunting and wriggling.

"Now! We can't let them get away!" yelled Jeremy.

The door began to close, and the plane began to glide towards the runway. Patsy broke cover and dashed towards it. Jeremy broke cover and decided that running after the thing was just too much effort.

A security guard approached the patrol car they'd been hiding behind, and hopped into the driver's seat. Jeremy hopped in beside him.

"Follow that plane!" he ordered.

"I can't do that," said the guard, "I'll be in trouble."

The plane was getting further away. Patsy's trainers pounded the tarmac. Her face was redder than her hair, and her arms shifted faster than a fresh batch of hot cakes.

"Quick!" said Jeremy. "Follow that plane!"

"Ooo, are you a secret agent or something?" said the guard excitedly.

"I can't tell you that, it's a secret!"

"Oh, go on, don't be rotten."

The plane's engines were picking up speed.

"Just drive!" yelled Jeremy.

The guard drove.

"You're not like the other guards, are you?" said Jeremy.

"No," said the guard sadly, "we don't get on very well."

The patrol car drew level with Patsy. If she'd been able to spare the time and energy to make a rude sign at Jeremy, she would have.

Faces appeared at the plane's windows. Sid looked horrified and shouted something to the pilot. The two Kenneths squashed their noses against the glass and puffed out their cheeks.

Patsy leaped forward, flinging herself on to the plane's wing. Her legs flapped madly as she fought to keep a grip on the smooth surface.

Jeremy wound down the window and clambered out on to the roof of the patrol car. The wind blew his hair into a frizzy mass, but there was no time to worry about that now. The guard swerved the patrol car nervously as Jeremy, flat on his stomach, crossed the roof. He pulled up his knees, steadied himself, and jumped.

He skidded across the wing. The plane was veering left and right in an effort to shake them off. Patsy caught his collar as he began to slip backwards. "Didn't I say I always have to save you?" she grumbled.

The door in the side of the plane *ksschunged* as it unlocked and swung open. Kenneth (they couldn't tell which one) stuck his head out. "Hello," he said with a little wave, "nice to see you again."

Sid kicked him from behind. "No it isn't!" he hissed. "Tell them to buzz off!"

"Buzz off," said Kenneth.

"No!" said Jeremy defiantly.

Sid's cackle was almost as loud as the engines. The door shut and bolted. The plane picked up speed, moving out on to the runway. It accelerated, faster and faster. Jeremy and Patsy gripped the wing with all their strength. Their eyes were tightly shut against the wind. The runway shot past under their feet. The whine of the engines rose higher and higher. The plane's nose rocked slightly. The runway seemed to drop away beneath them. The plane banked steeply upwards. Their stomachs suddenly rolled over and did a couple of double somersaults that any Olympic gymnast would have been proud of.

Kenneth and Kenneth watched calmly from inside. Second-Kenneth munched on a packet of wine gums. One day he'd learn to take the wine gums out first.

The plane gained altitude. Patsy's hands were frozen with cold and her face ached from being screwed up so hard.

"I— think—" she screamed at Jeremy, "when— they— said— buzz— off— you— should— have— said— YYEEEEESSSS!!"

Chapter 5

In which everybody gets duffed up and our heroes face certain death

Inside the plane, Sid dodged this way and that to see around the Kenneths. "What are they doing?" he said. "Why aren't they falling off?"

"That ginger lass is a strong 'un," murmured First-Kenneth to his brother. "I'd like her to be my girlfriend."

"Well, get out there and tell her, then!" spat Sid through gritted teeth.

"Huh?" said the Kenneths. Their jaws dangled.

"Get out on the wing and throw them off!" said Sid. "We've come too far to let a couple of do-gooders spoil things!" He turned, grinning weakly and bowing to the most unpleasant and disreputable computer thief in the world, who was sitting at the far end of the cabin. "Don't you agree, Your Most Wonderful Nastiness, Sir?" he squirmed.

The computer thief smiled a dreary smile.

Sid unlocked the door and flung it open. Howling blasts of air suddenly filled the cabin.

The first Jeremy and Patsy knew about Sid's plan was when two huge, heavy shapes thumped on to the wing in front of them. The plane spun to one side, the weight of all four of them pulling it over.

The Kenneths screamed for their mum. The ground, far below them, appeared to flip up and round and over their heads, and up and round and over as the plane rolled.

Jeremy and Patsy screamed for their mums too.

The Kenneths, holding on tightly, struck out. A fat palm smacked against Jeremy's shoulder and he let go with one hand. He fluttered like a shirt on a washing line. Patsy ducked to avoid a flying fist. She was sure she could hear someone shouting about going out for a pizza sometime, but decided she must be going barmy.

The plane stabilized, but on its side. The weight of the Kenneths kept the wing they were on pointing downwards, with the other wing sticking up vertically. Patsy glanced down for a second, then wished she hadn't. They were about ten thousand feet off the ground.

A fat fist smacked against Jeremy's fingers. Luckily, the fingers were so cold by now that the blow wasn't too painful, and he managed to hang on. Then a boot squashed into his face. His fingers were at full stretch. His mouth twisted sideways as the boot pushed harder.

Patsy's grip was being reduced a bit at a time. First-Kenneth grabbed each of her fingers in turn and pulled them off the surface of the wing. "One little piggy went to Margate..." called First-Kenneth. "One little piggy sat in foam..."

Jeremy yelled as loud as the boot would

allow: "Hey, boys! Who wants an ice cream?!"

The Kenneths both jumped up and down in excitement, then realized they were jumping up and down in mid-air. They found themselves watching the ground getting closer and closer.

With their weight gone, the plane flipped through one hundred and eighty degrees. Jeremy and Patsy's grip on the wing finally gave out and they, too, fell. But with the plane now the other way up, they fell straight in through the door. The plane twisted again and flew level.

Wind whipped around the cabin. Jeremy and Patsy painfully untangled themselves from the Eazee-Rest reclining seats, and stared up into Sid's weaselly face.

"Oh, I'm really, really unhappy now," said Sid quietly.

Jeremy clambered to his feet and tried to look dignified. "I order you to turn this plane around and return to the airport!"

"Shan't!" said Sid.

"Since they refuse to let us dispose of them," said a weary voice from the other end of the cabin, "they will have to come with us. We have many friends where we're going. They won't escape all of them."

Both Jeremy and Patsy knew that voice instantly.

There were lots of reasons why Jeremy liked being a secret agent. There was the thrill of bringing dangerous villains to justice, there was the joy of not being at school. There was also, now and again, the chance to be totally and completely gobsmacked by something. As the owner of the voice stood up and stepped forward, Jeremy could honestly say that his gob had never been more smacked. The mysterious figure at the airport had been Sharkface – definitely. However, the most unpleasant and disreputable computer thief in the world now turned out to be...

"Mr Plantaganet!" said Jeremy.

"Crumbs," said Patsy, peeking over the back of a seat.

"You're not the only one with a secret identity," said Mr Plantaganet dolefully. "I did a college course in computer piracy long ago, and with this," he pointed to the satellite, strapped firmly into a seat, "I can hack into any system anywhere in the world. Nothing will be safe. Not banks, not building society current accounts. I'll have access to money, anybody's and everybody's, whenever I want it."

Sid had read about this in the SCUM handbook – the big villain's revealing speech to the good guys, just before the end. He was filled with admiration. Then he frowned. Just before the end?

"Wait a minute!" he cried. "You're not getting *my* money!" The suitcase crammed with cash that Mr Plantaganet had given him in exchange for the satellite was wedged into the luggage rack overhead. Over Jeremy's head, fortunately. Jeremy yanked it free, intending to hold it up above him heroically, but it weighed a tonne. It thudded to the floor instead.

"Leave that alone, Brown!" cried Mr Plantaganet, with a weary sweep of his hand. "I've got to double-cross this little creep yet and steal it back!"

"*What??!*" yelled Sid.

"You pushed me into a swimming pool, you oaf!"

"Aha! You're not wearing your woolly jumper! I'm telling your mum!"

Jeremy kicked the case over and gave it a shove. It slid to the very edge of the open doorway. Sid and Mr Plantaganet both dived for it at the same time. Patsy pulled off a shoe and flung it hard. It hit the case, which toppled out into space, and the villains toppled out with it.

They fell trying to thump each other. The suitcase was snatched from one to the other and back again, as they shrank to tiny dots in the distance.

"I'm puzzled," said Jeremy. "That was Sharkface at the airport. Where did he go, then?"

"Look out!" yelled Patsy.

Sharkface sprang from the cockpit. He ripped a seat off its metal runners, and hurled it. They dropped to the floor and it crashed into the wall behind them.

"I suppose you've been the one piloting this thing," said Jeremy. Sharkface ripped up another seat.

"You're that snotty little Brown nobody from school," he grunted.

"I am Jeremy Brown of the Secret Service, and you're under arrest!"

Another seat smashed against the wall. Sharkface leaped at Jeremy. All Jeremy could think of was what had happened that morning on the way to school. He wasn't going to let it happen again. As Sharkface lunged for his throat, he ducked and rolled on to his back. Sharkface was going too fast to stop. He flew over Jeremy's head, and out through the door.

"That's that, then," said Jeremy.

Wrong.

The plane suddenly dipped sharply and went into a dive. The ground appeared through the front window, and the screaming of the engines rose to a deafening screech. Jeremy and Patsy tumbled forwards into the cockpit.

"Quick!" shouted Patsy. "Pull it up straight!"

Jeremy jumped into the pilot's seat and strapped himself in. His fingers fluttered over the dozens of switches and levers and displays in front of him. "Er..."

"You can fly a plane, can't you?" said Patsy. "I mean, Sharkface can fly a plane – *could* fly a plane. You must have done 'How to Fly a Plane' at MI7, surely?"

"That's next week," muttered Jeremy with a trembling voice.

"So this is it, then! After all that, we're still facing certain death!"

This time, one of Patsy's doom-laden remarks looked like being completely correct.

Jeremy grabbed the joystick in front of him and pulled hard. No response. He searched the displays for useful information. The ground was getting closer every second. A red light above a row of other red lights blinked: AUTOPILOT LOCKED. SECURITY CODE REQUIRED FOR RELEASE.

"Our history teacher taught Sharkface a trick or two, anyway," said Jeremy. "They've made sure that if they didn't make it, neither would we!"

"Would breaking anything help?" asked Patsy hopefully.

"No, no, no! Get the satellite!" said Jeremy. "We've been chasing it around all day, the least it can do for us is a few sums!"

Patsy struggled back up the cabin, which was now almost vertical. The engines howled, and the rushing air made the remaining seats shake violently. She unstrapped the satellite. The second the buckle was unfastened, the weight of the thing sent her (and it) crashing back into the cockpit.

"Don't damage it!" yelled Jeremy.

Patsy would have given him a poke in the eye if she hadn't been pinned flat against the control panel. Jeremy opened several hatches in the side of the satellite, unwound the electric leads that fell out, and searched for a suitable socket among the plane's controls, in front of him.

"The good thing about this technology stuff," he mumbled, "is that these days you can... Ahah!"

He plugged in. Patsy looked out of the window, then wished she hadn't. They couldn't have been more than five thousand feet off the ground now.

A screen came to life on the side of the satellite. As words appeared on it, a high, calm voice echoed them from a tiny speaker on the plane's control panel. "Initializing... Initializing..."

"Come on," mumbled Jeremy.

"Initialization stage complete," said the satellite gently. "Status now being checked."

"We're going to crash!! That's our bloomin' status!!" bellowed Patsy.

"Patsy, be cool," said Jeremy, very, very worried indeed.

"Status check complete," said the satellite calmly. "Altitude now 4,976 feet and falling... 4,532 feet and falling... 3,991 feet and falling... Speed beyond tolerance levels. Evasive action recommended."

"Well do it, then!" shouted Patsy.

"You can't just tell it, Patsy, you have to program it."

"3,433 feet."

Clouds flashed past the windows. Patsy could make out buildings down below. Her stomach said a quick toodle-oo and tried to find the nearest exit. Jeremy tapped uselessly at the keyboard set into the side of the satellite. It was at this point that he wished he'd paid more attention during Computer Science.

"2,877 feet," said the satellite. "Evasive action required. Impact in seventeen seconds ... sixteen ... fifteen ..."

"Shut up!!" screamed Patsy.

Jeremy clapped his hands to his head. He had to think. They both had to think. Thinking was the only way out.

"twelve ... eleven ... ten seconds ..."

"The satellite's monitoring the plane's controls now," murmured Jeremy quickly. "The controls are locked. If the satellite realizes they're locked, it'll take them over."

"nine ... eight ... seven ..."

Startled birds clung to the plane's nose, squawking. Patsy could see trees, fields, cars on the roads.

"six ... five ..."

Jeremy pulled hard on the joystick. The satellite bleeped.

"Controls disabled," it said soothingly. "Autopilot overridden. Safety program running."

Suddenly, the plane's nose lurched

upwards. Gravitational forces pulled Jeremy and Patsy tight into their seats. The plane swooped in a sharp U-shape. The tip of the left wing clipped a spray of leaves from a tree. The sudden falling of a whopping great aircraft, and its lightning manoeuvres back up into the sky, made a nearby flock of sheep jump out of their fleeces. Most of them would be taking pills for their nerves for the rest of their lives, but at least justice had been done, and a disaster averted.

As the plane automatically banked and headed back to the airport, Jeremy took out a hanky, mopped his brow, and had clearly forgotten all about the "How to Stop Shaking Like a Leaf" lesson MI7 had given him.

"Looks like I've saved the day again," he said cheerily.

Patsy socked him across the jaw, but he took no notice.

"Did I ever tell you about the time I fooled a Russian assassin into thinking he was a small dog called Arnold?"

"Yes," said Patsy crossly.

The concerned and sensitive reader will be pleased to hear that none of those ejected at ten thousand feet ended up as a blob of strawberry jam on someone's front doorstep. As the plane came safely in to land, Sid, the Kenneths, Mr Plantaganet and Sharkface were crawling safely out of the sludge tanks at the sewage works and into the welcoming arms of the airport security guards.

Jeremy and Patsy returned home. They trudged up the street towards their respective houses.

"I'm going to have a bath," said Jeremy. "I'm going to put these vilely stained clothes in the wash, and I'm going to prepare a new chapter for my memoirs, entitled 'I Foiled Crime at ten thousand Feet'."

Patsy said something very rude indeed, but Jeremy wasn't listening because there was a buzzing sensation in his left thumb…

JEREMY BROWN
AND THE
MUMMY'S CURSE

Chapter 1

In which Jeremy Brown shakes with fear and a mummy comes to life

....

Jeremy Brown's secret was safe. Everyone at Grotside School thought of him as that weedy kid with the glasses. Only his best friend, Patsy Spudd, knew that underneath the clever disguise, he was an MI7 agent. And a rather brilliant one at that, he always thought.

Of course, if he'd paid the same attention to his schoolwork as he did to catching crooks and saving the world, he'd have already got twelve A-levels, and a degree from the University of Brains. As it was, he came bottom in everything, unless Patsy beat him to it.

It was Friday afternoon, double Maths with Mr Algebra, and everyone was fed up.

"I'm fed up," mumbled Patsy, too fed up to

say anything more original. She kept curling her ginger hair around her fingers.

Mr Algebra wrote a set of formulae on the blackboard. If Jeremy had been paying attention, he'd have realized that they were perfect for helping to decode electronic locking systems. But he wasn't. Instead, he was thinking about his last mission, and how very clever he'd been in proving that diamonds were being smuggled out of the country by a little old lady from Swanage.

"Who'd have thought it," said Jeremy. "Hollow teeth."

"It was me who extracted them," said Patsy. "She might have been ninety-seven, but she still kicked like a mule," she added, rubbing her left leg.

The class stared vacantly at the blackboard with droopy eyes and ever droopier mouths. Some of them were bored to tears (and were wringing out their hankies), some of them were bored stupid (and had forgotten their names), but luckily none of them had been bored to death yet.

"I wish MI7 would call me with a case," muttered Jeremy. Very soon, he'd be wishing he hadn't said that. And to find out why, we must first go to Cairo...

The museum was dark, silent and smelled of old socks. It was the smell of thousands of years of ancient Egyptian history. Mummy cases lined the walls, and huge stone statues of gods and animals stood in every corner.

The last visitor of the day had left hours ago. Agent Spanner of MI7 wandered along the upper gallery of the main hall, keeping a sharp eye out for something he knew was there, somewhere. His footsteps echoed around the walls. He was wearing a smart white suit, which is probably the silliest thing you can wear in a hot, sticky climate like Egypt's, but he'd seen people wear them in films on the telly, so he reckoned he looked cool.

He dabbed the sweat off his forehead with his sleeve. It left a grubby stain. At last, he stopped in front of a particularly large, coffin-like and frightening-looking wooden sarcophagus. It was covered in ancient Egyptian hieroglyphics, and a large, noble face was painted near its top in black and gold. Agent Spanner gulped quietly. "The casket of Psidesalad II," he whispered.

With both hands gripping one edge of the lid, he heaved the mummy case open. It creaked and groaned. A scattering of dust puffed up and settled nervously around his feet, glad to be out of there.

The mummy, its arms folded across its chest, stood tall and terrifying before him. It was wrapped tightly in bandages, and the bandages were wrapped tightly in dirt.

"Eurgh, it's a bit mucky," he mumbled to himself.

A thin beam of blue light ran from one side of the case to the other, level with the mummy's knees. Carefully, Agent Spanner reached out and broke the beam with his fingers.

His scream of fright was, just at that moment, the loudest noise in Cairo. The mummy's tightly encased hands had jerked into life. With sudden, sharp movements it grabbed the sides of the case and hauled itself forward.

Agent Spanner jumped back. The mummy's feet landed with twin thuds on the stone floor. He jumped back some more. The mummy stood up straight, towering over him. Agent Spanner would have liked to jump back roughly as far as France, but he was now pressed tightly against an exhibit of primitive farming tools.

The mummy closed in. Agent Spanner's eyes bulged out of his face like golf balls sitting on a pizza...

Jeremy's eyes were also bulging. He'd fixed his lids open with sticky tape in an effort to look alert, but all it was doing was making his eyes water.

"Did I tell you about when I had to glue

my knees together to prop a bank vault door open?"

"Many times," sighed Patsy.

Suddenly, Jeremy's tie began to make a tiny beeping noise. He sat up straight, wide awake. The rest of the class turned to peer sleepily at him. Mr Algebra craned his neck and shuffled from side to side. "Brown? Are you emitting a peculiar noise?"

Jeremy thought quickly. "Er, yes sir. It's my lower intestine. Very embarrassing personal problem, sir. Could erupt any minute."

Mr Algebra shuffled in horror at the thought of his lovely classroom awash with… "Quick! Get out! Find the school nurse! Or a toilet!"

"Thank you, sir," said Jeremy. All but one member of the class giggled cruelly as he dashed for the door. The odd one out was, of course, Patsy. She knew very well what that beeping meant.

Outside, in the chalky corridor, Jeremy quickly checked that nobody could see him.

He stuck one end of his tie into his ear
(the end with the miniature speaker in it)
and held the other close to his mouth
(the end with the miniature microphone).

"The fairy cakes are made of sponge," said
the deep voice of his boss at MI7.

"With big red cherries on the top,"
responded Jeremy correctly. "Morning,
boss."

"Good morning, Agent Brown. Pay
attention. A week ago, we lost contact
with one of our overseas operatives, Agent
Wrench. He'd been sent to Egypt, to guard
an exhibition of relics on loan from the
British Museum. After several days of silence,
we sent a second operative, Agent Spanner,
to track him down. Spanner discovered local
reports of an ancient curse, which Agent
Wrench had apparently fallen victim to."

Jeremy was starting to get a sinking feeling.
"And what happened then?"

"No idea. Spanner vanished too.
Swallowed up by the curse of the pharaoh

Psidesalad II, by all accounts."

"Oh." It was at this point that Jeremy began shaking with fear, as mentioned at the start of the chapter.

"Your mission," continued the boss, "is to go to Egypt, find out what's going on and stop it."

"I see… Er, wouldn't this be better tackled by … someone … a bit … taller, maybe?"

"Sorry, Brown. Every other agent is off on a training exercise – 'How to Confuse Your Enemies With a Garden Hose'. You're the only one left. Operation Exit will be launched, as normal."

Jeremy's secret radio beeped, spluttered and switched off. Moments later, the bell for the end of the lesson shattered the silence, not to mention his nerves. His legs wobbled and gave way of their own accord. As he got up off the floor and tried to look dignified, Patsy appeared at his side.

"I take it we're off?" she said eagerly.

His everyday disguise was redundant once

more. Time for Jeremy to stop looking weedy and scruffy and start looking all heroic and smart. He straightened his tie, pulled up his socks and put on his special eagle-eyed look. Then he gave Patsy a quick summary of the situation. "MI7 chose me specially," he said. "The others all wanted the job, but there's only me brilliant enough to tackle it, of course."

"We're off, then!" Patsy grinned.

Operation Exit, meanwhile, involved MI7 telephoning the Headmaster of Grotside School. He was told that he should sign a letter allowing both of them to be out of lessons for as long as they wanted, otherwise the world would get to hear about his visits to the Peter Pixie Dressing-Up Club.

Jeremy and Patsy collected their letter from his trembling hands on the way out of the school gates and hurried to the airport. They flew to Cairo in the time it takes to start a new chapter.

Chapter 2

In which Jeremy, Patsy and a camel are shot at with poison darts

....

It was hot. Very, very hot. Think of the wave of heat you get when the oven door is opened. It was hotter than that.

"Oooh, it's hot," said Jeremy. He and Patsy had taken a taxi from Cairo Airport, but after the taxi driver had made them give it back, they'd caught the bus. They had now arrived at a busy, dusty, noisy and quite amazingly hot bus station outside the famous Museum of Antiquities.

Patsy had remembered to bring her wide-brimmed sunhat, and had it jammed tightly on her head, but Jeremy had to keep squinting. A short, round man wearing trendy sunglasses and what looked like an enormous nightshirt came bustling out of the museum and shook their hands warmly.

Patsy was going to make a joke about pyjamas, but didn't. "It's not a nightshirt, it's called a gallibiyya," whispered Jeremy. "Traditional Arab dress."

"Sheik Yabelli," said the round man, with a broad grin. Jeremy and Patsy looked at each other for a moment, then realized that this was his name. "I'm in charge of the British Museum exhibits while they're here in Egypt," he said.

"I am Jeremy Brown of the Secret Service," announced Jeremy in his most official-sounding voice. "And this is my Operations Co-ordinator, Patsy Spudd."

CrunCHH-chomp!

Patsy spun around, ready to thump whoever had just snatched her hat away. She found herself staring up into the face of a dopey-looking camel. The last shreds of her hat were just vanishing between its teeth.

"This is my camel, Deidre," said Sheik Yabelli proudly. "Say hello, Deidre."

Deidre snorted loudly at Patsy. Patsy wiped her face clean, grumbling rudely under her breath.

"I named her Deidre in honour of my favourite aunt," said the Sheik.

"Why, does your aunt like camels?" asked Jeremy.

"No, she just looks like one," said the Sheik. "MI7 informed me you'd be arriving. In view of the fact that the curse of Psidesalad II has already gobbled up two of your agents, I have arranged a bodyguard for you."

Two pairs of piercing, narrow eyes darted into view, behind which lurked the Sheik's henchmen, Mustafa and Dontafa. They, too, wore long, flowing gallibiyyas. Patsy thought they looked like they'd both sell their grannies for half a dozen trading cards and a jam doughnut. Jeremy just thought they were terrifying.

"Hello, boys," he said, with a polite but wobbly smile.

Mustafa and Dontafa bowed low, and said nothing. It was lucky that their bows almost brought their noses to ground level, because otherwise they'd have been hit by the poison darts which now flew over their backs.

Patsy kicked Jeremy hard on the hip, and he was thrown sideways. The darts missed his shoulder by millimetres and embedded themselves into the side of a passing wooden cart.

"Ow!" yelled Jeremy.

"You'd have been oww-ing worse than that if they'd hit you!" said Patsy. "Look!"

As the cart disappeared into the crowds, they could see that the wood around the area where the darts had struck was turning black.

"Poisoned," said Jeremy quietly. "Where did they come from?"

Phhh-eeoooo! Phhh-eeoooo! Two more bounced off the pavement by their feet. Mustafa and Dontafa were suddenly nowhere to be seen. Sheik Yabelli was spinning on the spot, looking this way and that.

Jeremy remembered what he'd read in MI7's "How to Spot Trouble" brochure. He quickly analysed his surroundings: lots of people, lots of cars and three really enormous camels. Much bigger than Deidre. And sort of ... shiny-looking!

The head of one of the big camels suddenly swivelled round. Its perfectly round eyes zoomed in on him. Where there should have been pupils, there were cross hairs, like the rangefinder of a gun. The camel's head jutted forward. Slots slid open across its nostrils.

Phhh-eeoooo! Phhh-eeoooo! Jeremy dropped to the dusty pavement. The darts whizzed over his head.

"They're after us!" he yelled at Patsy. Now he'd got his shirt all grubby, and that made things even worse as far as he was concerned.

Patsy began to make a dash for it, but there was too much traffic. Every direction was blocked with people, buses, taxis, carts and market stalls!

Phhh-eeoooo! Phhh-eeoooo! Smack into the

front tyre of a bicycle. The rider pitched over into the back of a truck-load of manure, which carried him away with his legs wriggling wildly in the air.

A dart could hit one of the crowd at any moment! Jeremy had an idea.

"Sheik!" he called. "Can we borrow Deidre?"

Sheik Yabelli had taken cover under Ibrahim's Pet Parade stall, behind a sign saying LITTLE BIRDIES, GOING CHEAP. His hand poked out in a quick thumbs-up sign.

The three big camels were marching through the crowd, heads turning, target sensors homing in on Jeremy and Patsy. Their legs whirred and *ka-clunk*ed as they walked.

"Are they what I think they are?" whispered Patsy.

"Yes," said Jeremy. "Robot camels with nasal armaments!"

Patsy jumped up onto Deidre's back and hauled Jeremy up after her. Remembering her camel driving lessons, she tugged on Deidre's ears. "Move!" she bellowed. Deidre lurched and bucked.

The robots instantly turned to pursue them, walking faster.

Deidre, not being the most intelligent animal in the world, bounded ahead in a straight line, and bounding ahead in a straight line meant going right over the roofs of the cars. Jeremy and Patsy hung on as best they could. Deidre crunched her way across one vehicle after another, closely followed by various threats of legal action, and beheading.

The robots increased their speed. They took a different approach with the traffic. They kicked it out of the way. A taxi was hurled over the railings of the museum. The fleeing crowd was splattered with bits of squashed fruit from a shattered cart.

Patsy tugged on Deidre's right ear, and the camel took a sharp turn down a narrow sidestreet lined with shops. The way ahead was more or less clear, and Deidre got up to a full gallop. The sound of cars being crunched was close behind them.

Back in the street, an enormous lorry, carrying rocks, skidded and crushed one of the robots under its wheels. The robot's casing split, showering the street with sparks and circuits. The remaining two ignored it. They turned right, down the sidestreet.

Jeremy took a quick glance back. The robots were galloping too, and much faster than Deidre. They'd catch up in seconds. Their heads jutted forward, and their nostrils whirred open.

"Who's controlling them?" shouted Patsy.

"I could make a couple of guesses!" shouted Jeremy. "But right now I'm more worried about the—"

Phhh-eeoooo! Phhh-eeoooo!

Dozens of darts buzzed through the air. Jeremy and Patsy dodged left and right, gripping tightly on to Deidre's tough, shaggy coat (which was so tough and shaggy that darts simply bounced off it). Deidre galloped as fast as she could, her tongue lolling out. Her wet, slobbery lips flapped in the wind.

Phhh-eeoooo! Phhh-eeoooo! Darts struck the canvas awnings of some of the shops. Shoppers and shopkeepers dived out of the way. The robots moved faster, and faster. Jeremy could smell the engine oil in their joints.

Oil! Something slippery! Jeremy looked up the street, which wasn't easy with Deidre bumping and weaving all over the place. Ahead was a large stall selling shampoo and soap.

"Patsy!" called Jeremy. "Hair gel!"

"Can't you forget your bloomin' hair for once?" cried Patsy. Then she realized what he meant. She gave a sharp nod, held on extra tight around Deidre's neck with her legs and flung herself sideways. As they shot past the stall, she reached out and plucked off a

jumbo-sized tub of gel. The weight of
it almost dragged her under Deidre's
thundering feet. She grunted and struggled,
and pulled herself back upright, then quickly
handed the tub to Jeremy.

A dart *peee-oww*ed through the shoulder
of Jeremy's blazer, turning a little patch of it
black. Now he was REALLY cross. Taking aim
as accurately as possible (which meant not at
all accurately, in the circumstances), he flung
the tub of gel.

It spun in a neat arc and burst with a
sloppy *splop* on the ground. The robot that
was bringing up the rear stepped straight in
it. Its legs buckled and slipped. It flipped
helplessly head over heels, smacked into a
wall and exploded in a deafening clap of
thunder and a ball of flame.

The other robot ignored it, and carried
on running.

"I bet this sort of thing never happens to
the tourists," grumbled Patsy.

*   *   *

A group of thirty-two tourists, on a package tour organized by Sun & Sand Holidays Ltd, were at that moment enjoying a leisurely sightseeing cruise down the River Nile. The Sun & Sand representative was speaking to them slowly and calmly:

"So here we are, on the Nile, in the centre of bustling Cairo, the capital of Egypt. On your left, fishing boats, known as feluccas. On your right, busy streets full of shops where you can buy souvenirs and ..." (a puzzled pause) "racing camels?"

The tourists turned, curious. Sure enough a camel, carrying two Europeans, had just shot out from one of the narrow sidestreets.

Up ahead, the end of the street was in sight.

"The river!" shouted Jeremy. "We can short-circuit it!"

Patsy grinned gleefully. She was going to enjoy this bit.

The last robot was right behind them. Darts rained down around Deidre's feet.

The tourists watched silently as a real camel, followed by a robot one, leaped at high speed off the tall bank of the Nile. The real camel hit their boat feet first. The robot tumbled into the water.

The weight of the real camel smashed through the seats, smashed a hole in the boat's bottom, and deposited Jeremy and Patsy on top of the Sun & Sand representative. The boat sank. Mrs Bedsit (from Hull) screamed at the top of her voice. Mr Bungalow (from Leamington Spa) was knocked unconscious by a lump of flying robot.

The water flooded the robot's gears and blew all its circuits. Like the boat, it quickly sank out of sight.

"I think we gave them the hump," said Jeremy.

Deidre doggy-paddled, or rather camel-paddled, to the shore. The tourists demanded their money back.

Chapter 3

In which darkness falls, and so does a sarcophagus

....

Two hours later, four things had happened.
1) Deidre had been returned to Sheik Yabelli,
safe and sound. 2) News of the camel attack
had spread, creating fearful whispers
throughout Cairo about the curse of
Psidesalad II. 3) The sun had set, and long,
black shadows had crept through the streets,
beneath a sky streaked with a fiery red.
4) Jeremy had put on a clean shirt.

The Sheik had found Jeremy and Patsy
rooms at the remarkably large and
remarkably shiny Pyramids Palace Hotel.
They checked in wearing dark glasses and
false beards, and using the fake identities
of Mr N. Code and Miss D. Cypher.

"Lucky I'm a master of disguise," said
Jeremy. "Nobody will guess we're undercover
agents now. Whoever sent the robot camels

after us might be searching the hotels, so we must be careful."

They had dinner in the hotel's remarkably posh restaurant, hiding behind their menus. Jeremy had an exotic mix of traditional Eastern dishes – mazzah to start, then kusheri and fattah, followed by baklava. Patsy had pie and chips.

"I can't take you anywhere," grumbled Jeremy.

"I like chips," hissed Patsy through gritted teeth.

With the moon high in the sky, they made their way to the museum. The Sheik had lent them a key. Jeremy wasn't keen on wandering around a dark and mysterious old building in the middle of the night, especially when there were ancient curses lurking about the place. However, Patsy called him a big weedy weed, and he changed his mind.

The huge, wooden front door shut with a clangorous thud behind them. The sound echoed off the massive stone pillars that rose up high into the gloom, then got hopelessly lost among the statues and glass cases. Jeremy switched on the torch they'd also borrowed from the Sheik.

"This place smells of old socks," mumbled Patsy, wrinkling her nose up.

Jeremy examined a small figurine of a jackal-headed god. "Should have paid more attention in History," he said. "Now then, time to bring my simply enormous brainpower into play and find some clues."

Patsy pulled an uh-oh-here-we-go face. Jeremy pretended he hadn't seen.

"Do we have a clear idea of exactly what's going on?" he said.

"No," said Patsy.

"Have we got any firm leads on what might have happened to Agent Wrench and Agent Spanner?"

"No," said Patsy.

"So, we're not doing too badly, so far, are we?"

"No," said Patsy.

A sharp beam of torchlight wobbled ahead of them as they tiptoed around the displays, up a wide stone staircase, along a narrow corridor, through a room filled with manuscripts, past a model of an ancient Egyptian village ... and realized they were completely lost. Then they remembered the map that they'd also borrowed from the Sheik, and soon arrived at the tall, vaulted gallery where the mummy cases stood.

Jeremy ran the torch beam up and down each case. They didn't get much of a look at the beautiful designs and skilful carvings on them, because his hand was shaking with fright.

"Oh, give it here," said Patsy, pulling the torch away from him.

"This one over here must be one of the exhibits from London. This is the sarcophagus of Psidesalad II," whispered Patsy.

Jeremy gazed up at it, his eyes nearly as wide open as his mouth. "How do you know?" he breathed. "Can you read the hieroglyphics on the casing?"

"No, I can read the label on the side which says PROPERTY OF THE BRITISH MUSEUM. Shine the torch here, along the floor."

There were footprints and marks in the dust, all over the wooden boards. Hundreds of visitors had passed this spot in the last few days, but Jeremy picked out two sets of prints which came closer to the sarcophagus than all the others.

"Look," he whispered. "One pair of ordinary-sized feet, one pair so big they'd make King Kong wet his pants. The ordinary feet jump backwards, away from the others, as if they're trying to escape." (These were Agent Spanner's footprints, as made on page 92.)

"How do you know they're going backwards?" asked Patsy.

"Because they go right up to this glass

exhibit case, but they're facing away from it. Whoever it was – maybe Agent Wrench or Agent Spanner – clearly didn't walk through the glass case and towards the sarcophagus. The glass case is full and unbroken. So he must have been going backwards from the sarcophagus to the glass case. See?"

Patsy didn't. "You mean he came out of the sarcophagus?" she said, puzzled.

"No, the enormous footprints come out of the sarcophagus," said Jeremy.

They looked at each other for a second. Shivery sensations gleefully played football in their stomachs. Without a sound, Patsy shone the torch along the side of the sarcophagus. There wasn't a trace of dust along its edge.

"Recently opened," gulped Jeremy.

"We'd better take a look inside," said Patsy.

"We'd better call MI7 for back-up. Tanks, cars with sirens, that sort of thing."

"No time," said Patsy. She gripped the edge of the mummy case and heaved it open. It creaked and groaned. The torch lit up the tightly bandaged face of the mummy inside. Its arms were crossed over its chest, and it towered above them.

"Big bloke, wasn't he?" trembled Jeremy.

With a sudden rush of fear to the head, Patsy slammed the lid shut again. As you may have guessed, she was a lass who was stronger than she looked, and the force of the slam made the whole sarcophagus wobble dangerously. Their efforts to stop its rocking motion only managed to make things worse.

"Jump!" yelled Patsy. "It's coming down."

They dodged sideways as the heavy wooden case hit the floor with a shattering crunch. It instantly split into a hundred pieces.

The shattering crunch's echo died away, and the dust began to settle. In the shaky torchlight, they could see the mummy lying face down in the debris. Was that the sound of the broken pieces settling? Or were they being moved aside? Was that the moon throwing eerie shadows across the room?

Or was the mummy trying to stand up?

"Oh, crumbs," whispered Jeremy.

It was unmistakable now. With slow, jerky movements, the mummy was clambering to its feet. Pieces of sarcophagus were swept away with casual swats of its chunky, wrapped hands. As it reached its full height, it turned to face them. Its arms reached out for them.

"I think," said Patsy, "that this is the bit where we RUUUUUUNN!"

In their fright, they ran into each other, and various exhibits, as much as they ran for the exit. Not that they knew where the exit was any more – the map was somewhere under all that mess.

The mummy lurched forwards, straight at them. They turned a corner and found themselves in a long room lined with mummy cases. The sound of slow, heavy footsteps thudded in the darkness behind them.

"I've got a brilliant idea," said Jeremy. "But it's revolting, so I won't tell you what it is."

"Hide in the mummy cases!" cried Patsy. "Brilliant!"

"Eurgh!" squirmed Jeremy.

"They're only dead bodies!" said Patsy. "Or would you rather be got by King Tut back there?"

They each chose a sarcophagus, and hauled the lids open. Leaping inside, however, was not an option. Bandaged arms instantly lunged at them. Mummies, every bit as huge as the first one, stepped out. The lids of the other cases in the room slowly creaked open.

Jeremy and Patsy turned and dashed back the way they had come. Then they realized that the first mummy was back that way, so instead they turned and dashed along the gallery which overlooked the main hall.

"This is where commando combat training comes in handy," gasped Jeremy.

"Yes. If only you'd had some," said Patsy.

Fortunately, the stairs down to the hall were straight ahead of them. Unfortunately, up the stairs were coming half a dozen more mummies. Jeremy and Patsy skidded to a halt.

"Trapped!" said Patsy.

Jeremy leaned over the gallery's railings, looking down into the gloom of the hall. They couldn't simply jump over – too high. He ran over to the nearest exhibits – a statue that was far too heavy to move, a mummified cat and an oar from an ancient boat.

The mummies closed in on both sides. The thumping of their enormous feet made the floor shake.

Jeremy grabbed the mummified cat and started to unravel its bandages. He tied one end around the railings.

"I hope this moggie was well fed," he said. "We need enough wrappings to climb down at least thirty metres!"

Patsy quickly wound out the wrappings over the edge, tying loose ends together as she went. She nearly mentioned something about these strips of cloth being two thousand years old and therefore unlikely to take their weight, but she didn't. She soon wished she had.

The mummies emerged from the shadows. They were barely an arm's length away. A mummy's arm's length, that is.

"Move!" yelled Patsy. Clinging on tightly, the two of them launched themselves over the railings, and dropped. Two of the mummies swung their fists, but only succeeded in hitting each other. The one closest to the railings was knocked over them.

Jeremy and Patsy fell for the height of two double-decker buses before the cat's wrappings reached their limit and pulled tight. Sure enough, two-thousand-year-old strips of cloth are complete rubbish when it comes to dangling in mid-air from a railing. They snapped instantly, but the sudden jerk that snapped them was also enough to break Jeremy's and Patsy's fall. They hit the stone floor of the main hall with a variety of painful thuds, but fortunately with no bones broken.

The falling mummy almost landed on top of them, making dents and cracks in the floor. Its innards made a crashing, coming-apart-at-the-seams noise. The bandages around its right arm came loose, revealing shiny metal beneath.

"They're robots too!" said Patsy.

"Thought as much," fibbed Jeremy. "I, er … never believed all that curse business, anyway."

The other mummies were now lumbering down the stairs. Jeremy and Patsy hurriedly untangled themselves from the heap of wrappings and bits of smashed robot that littered the floor. Without looking back – without looking anywhere, really, because it was especially dark down here – they scrambled for the front door.

The damage they caused by bumping into things and knocking them over was nothing compared to the damage caused by the mummies bumping into things and knocking them over.

With the sound of pounding feet and disintegrating relics ringing in their ears, Jeremy and Patsy flung open the door and ran across the museum gardens. The mummies were still in pursuit, crowding through the door and spreading out to cover the grounds.

Jeremy and Patsy jumped onto the back of a passing horse and cart. Jeremy was relieved to find that it was carrying rolls of cloth, and not something smelly.

"Good evening," he called politely to the sleepy driver. "Could I possibly ask you to drive us away from here very, very fast indeed?"

The driver turned, rubbing his eyes. "Huh?" he grunted. Then he caught sight of the mummies. Pausing only for him to scream, the cart shot away into the night.

Chapter 4

In which Patsy is nearly sick, and Jeremy uses his comb

··

The cup shook, and the tea in the cup shook in time with it, and all because Sheik Yabelli's hand was shaking too. As he held the cup delicately, his little finger poked out at an angle, and that was shaking worst of all.

The Sheik, Jeremy and Patsy were sitting on big fluffy cushions, in a neatly ordered room in the Sheik's house. It was early the next morning. Patsy hadn't yet noticed that Deidre (curled up on a carpet behind her) was nibbling at her hair. Household staff wandered back and forth, doing the laundry, tidying up and listening in on the conversation.

"A most interesting story, Mr Brown," said the Sheik, adjusting his sunglasses.

"It appears that our museum, our pride and joy, has been taken over by monsters."

"Robots," corrected Patsy.

"Still monsters in my book," said the Sheik. He took a nervous slurp of tea. Jeremy and Patsy did the same. "And they are beginning to move around throughout the city," he continued. "Nobody will take action against them. Not even the army. The power of the ancient curse is upon us."

"The power of MI7 will be upon us if we don't get to the bottom of all this," said Jeremy. "For a start, where are those two bodyguards you assigned to us?"

"Mustafa and Dontafa?" said the Sheik. "They vanished too. Right off the street, as you were chased by those devil-camels!"

Deidre gave a shudder at the memory of them, and the shudder pulled a chunky tuft out of Patsy's hair. Patsy slapped her hands to the back of her head, and spun around, glaring.

Jeremy's eyes went all shifty and his voice went all suspicious. "Of course," he said, "whoever is controlling the robots would want to make it look like they'd vanished too."

The Sheik gulped down the last of his tea. "Perhaps you're right. I never quite trusted those two. Come, I have my helicopter on standby on the roof. The streets will not be safe."

"Hey, Patsy," said Jeremy. "Helicopters. Your favourite."

But Patsy wasn't listening. She was too busy fighting with Deidre on the carpet.

The sun beat down as the helicopter rose. The Sheik was the pilot because he liked to be the one to say all that "Roger, over and out" stuff into the radio. Jeremy was beside him, binoculars at the ready. Patsy and Deidre were on the back seat. Patsy made rude signs at Deidre, and Deidre licked Patsy's face.

"I think I'm going to be sick," growled Patsy.

The helicopter swooped over Cairo. The Sheik liked to be the one to do all that swooping stuff, too.

They could see broad, flat roofs, tiny streets, the domes of the historic mosques in the old part of the city. And it was all a sort of light brown colour. Possible puns about a Brown being in a brown place were completely ignored. Jeremy scanned the city through his binoculars.

"It's very dark down there," he said. Patsy leaned over and took the lens caps off. "Ah, but I think I'm looking at a better angle now. I can see … some people running… And over there I can see … some other people running… Mummies are after them… They're running towards each other… They've … run into each other… The mummies are still after them… They're scattering…" He put down his binoculars. "Isn't it interesting, watching the way they go in all directions like that?"

"I think they'd prefer it if we actually helped them," said Patsy, trying to clean Deidre's dribble off her ear with a hanky.

"Quite right," said Jeremy. "We must map the robots' movements. Sheik, time to do some more of that swooping stuff, if you'd be so kind."

"Brill!" said the Sheik, and set about banking and swerving the helicopter, first in one direction, then another. Jeremy peered through his binoculars at the streets below and scribbled notes onto the back of his hand. Patsy clung to her seat for dear life. Deidre had a sneezing fit in Patsy's face.

"I really am going to be sick!" shouted Patsy, getting out her hanky again.

The helicopter swooped and dived, sometimes in order to fly over a new area of the city but mostly because the Sheik was really enjoying himself. Jeremy kept a careful count of where mummies were to be seen (at regular intervals, every two or three streets), and in which direction they were heading (the same direction, on the whole). Before long, he came to the conclusion that they'd been set out to form –

"A barrier," he said.

The MI7 book *How to Impress People*, which Jeremy had read several times, stated that now was the point at which any non-MI7 personnel present should ask an interesting question. Patsy was too busy avoiding Deidre's bad breath by pressing her hands over her face, so Sheik Yabelli stepped in and did the honours. "You mean they're protecting something?" he said.

"Precisely," said Jeremy, impressively. "They're in a roughly semicircular formation and they're moving very slowly in that direction." He pointed ahead of them. "Which means that whatever they're protecting will be in *that* direction!" He pointed behind them.

Sheik Yabelli swung the helicopter around. Directly ahead of them now, rising high above the rooftops, were three gigantic triangles.

"The pyramids," murmured Jeremy.

"The pyramids don't need protecting," said the Sheik. "They're big enough to look after themselves."

Jeremy got on with a bit of careful thinking. The helicopter flew out over the wide area of sand which separated the city from the pyramids. Deidre got ready for a really huge, nostril-cleaning sneeze.

Patsy shut her eyes tightly. "If we don't land *now*, I am *going to be sick*!"

The helicopter rapidly descended.

The group of thirty-two tourists, on a package tour organized by Sun & Sand Holidays Ltd, were at that moment enjoying a guided tour of the area which separated the city from the pyramids. They hadn't been told about the patrolling mummies. They also hadn't got over having their river cruise ruined by falling camels in Chapter Two, but the company had persuaded them not to fly home and complain to the authorities. The Sun & Sand representative was speaking to them slowly and calmly:

"So here we are, next to the magnificent pyramids, one of the ancient wonders of the world. On your left, the giant Sphinx, a human-headed statue of a lion. On your right, many charming little stalls where you can buy souvenirs and ..." (a puzzled pause) "helicopters?"

The tourists turned, curious. Sure enough, a helicopter was rapidly descending towards them. For a few moments, they looked at each other, and then they looked at the Sun & Sand rep. That delay was their big mistake.

The violent downdraft caused by the helicopter's rotors blasted sand, souvenirs and tourists in all directions. The area was engulfed in a whirlwind. Mrs Bedsit (from Hull) screamed at the top of her voice. Mr Bungalow (from Leamington Spa) was knocked unconscious by a flying souvenir stall. The Sun & Sand rep began to cry.

Patsy leaped out of the helicopter, closely followed by Jeremy, who was a bit annoyed at the way the whirlwind kept messing up his hair. Deidre, not having thumbs, was unable to undo her seat belt, and so she stayed where she was. With a cheery wave, the Sheik guided the helicopter back up into the sky, and with a quick loop-the-loop vanished into the distance.

"Which pyramid shall we try first?" said Patsy.

"We must apply careful, deductive methods to the situation," said Jeremy, combing his hair. "Let's see… Eeny, meeny, miny, mo…"

They set off for the one in the middle. The one on the right was the biggest, and therefore too obvious as a hiding place, and the one on the left was a long way away.

"It's too hot to walk," grumbled Jeremy.

Behind them, the tourists were fighting

their way out from under mountains of sand and bits of shredded souvenir stall.

"Wow," said Patsy.

The gigantically enormous shape of the pyramid rose way up high in front of them. It was made of massive stone blocks, each the size of a wardrobe. There were a number of openings at various points up the sloping side.

"Entrances to the tombs of the pharaoh and his queen," said Jeremy. "Originally, they were sealed up, but the passageways were excavated long ago."

"Wow," said Patsy.

Shielding his eyes from the dazzling sunlight, Jeremy craned his neck to examine the entrances. Patsy kept getting a nervous tingle down her spine. It might have been leftover drops of Deidre's dribble, but it was more probably a feeling of creeping unease.

"Better get a move on," she said "Those mummies could turn up at any minute."

"There!" said Jeremy, pointing to an entrance about halfway up the pyramid. "They're in there. All the other entrances are worn at the edges, but that one's cut nice and sharp into the stone."

"So it must be new," said Patsy.

"Right," said Jeremy. "You know, sometimes my brilliance astounds even me!"

Patsy began to clamber up the stone blocks. Jeremy tried to think of a way to ascend without having to get all hot and bothered, but he couldn't.

By the time they'd hauled themselves up level with the entrance, they were hotter and more bothered than Jeremy had dared fear. They looked back down, but that just made them feel dizzy as well. Up here, the breeze made spooky noises as it whistled around the stones, and would have pulled creepy faces too, had it been able. They stared through the entrance into the pitch-black tunnel ahead of them.

"A-a-after you," said Jeremy.

With a quick oh-for-goodness'-sake look, Patsy marched in. Jeremy tiptoed. What neither of them knew was that it didn't matter how they proceeded. They had already been detected by an electronic early warning system, and a trapdoor was being activated.

All they could see, as they edged down the passageway, was a rectangle of sky slowly getting smaller behind them. They felt their way delicately along the smooth, cold walls. The floor was angled steeply downwards, and they could feel scatterings of sand beneath their feet.

"The robots must come in and out along here," whispered Jeremy.

"It seems pretty quiet at the moment," whispered Patsy. "Perhaps we can creep up behind them undetected."

"I reckon so," whispered Jeremy. "Looks like they've underestimated our keen intelligence and fiendish cunning."

KA-CHUNGGGG!
"WhoaaaAAAAAAAAAaaaaaa!"
"WheeeeeaaaaEEEEEEEEEEE!"
That was the trapdoor.

Chapter 5

In which the villains are unmasked, and our heroes are done for, for sure

····································

"Begin second stage production line!"

The voice was low, echoing around the shadowy, cavernous chamber. It came from a speaker mounted on the wall, above a line of complex-looking machines. Jeremy and Patsy were rubbing whatever bits of themselves they'd bashed on the way down the metal chute which had been lurking under the trapdoor.

"I knew I should have worn standard issue MI7 padded underpants," said Jeremy, wincing.

Suddenly, a mummy appeared out of the shadows. They froze with fear, but quickly thawed out again when they realized that it wasn't interested in doing them any damage.

It lumbered across to one of the machines, pressed a sequence of buttons, and pulled a small red lever. The machine shuddered and clunked into life, and was soon chugging away to itself, emitting the occasional hiss of steam. The mummy went on its way.

As their eyes got used to the dimness, Jeremy and Patsy could make out many such machines, arranged in rows. Between the machines trundled conveyor belts, carrying various mechanical components. In the centre of the cavern rose a series of thick pipes, feeding into a huge cone-shaped device, which was suspended above the floor, pointing down.

"It's a factory," said Jeremy. "And you don't have to be as fabulously clever as me to work out what it's making."

"How long do you reckon it'll take to make an entire robot army?" said Patsy.

"Better ask Mustafa and Dontafa," said Jeremy. "I'm convinced those so-called bodyguards are behind all this. Even the Sheik said he didn't trust them."

"Well, now's your chance," said Patsy.

Jeremy turned in the direction Patsy was pointing. There, in a glass-sided booth marked PRISONERS, bound tightly with ropes, blindfolded and gagged, were Mustafa and Dontafa. Jeremy began to suspect that he might possibly have been wrong.

"Maybe they're bluffing," he said grumpily.

"Or maybe," said a smarmy voice behind them, "we've caught another pair of nosy parkers."

Jeremy and Patsy were surrounded by mummies. Above the mummies, standing on one of the chugging machines, were Agent Spanner and Agent Wrench. Jeremy couldn't help noticing that their smart white suits had become all wrinkled and marked in the heat of the desert.

"I told Spanner to buy more practical attire, but he wouldn't listen," slimed Agent Wrench. He sneered at the glass booth.

"These two tracked down our robot camel storage depot, and now, Brown, you and your scruffy little friend can join them in the cage. It will then be lowered into a pit of fresh concrete, from which you might possibly be rescued in a thousand years or so."

"And just where are you going to get a pit of fresh concrete?" cried Patsy.

Agent Wrench wriggled a long finger, flipped a switch on the side of one of the machines and, with an electric hum, a door slid open in the floor. "Here's one I prepared earlier." He grinned horribly. He turned to Agent Spanner. "Spanner, I'm going to check the production line. Get the mummies to deal with these two."

"Do I have to?" whined Agent Spanner. "Those mummies frighten the life out of me."

"Yes, you do!" yelled Wrench. "What kind of a criminal mastermind are you, if you can't send a few do-gooders to a nasty death! Get on with it!"

He scurried away. Agent Spanner waved in the general direction of Jeremy and Patsy. "Umm, stick them in the concrete, mummies, if you don't mind, please," he said.

The mummies lunged, and grabbed our heroes. Jeremy and Patsy were sealed up in the glass booth, along with their bodyguards, before Jeremy could think of a single witty remark.

"We're done for, for sure," quivered Patsy.

"Er..." said Jeremy.

With a jerk, the booth was hoisted into the air. It shook violently, but it was mostly the prisoners who were doing the shaking. The oozy, grey rectangle in the floor was directly below them. The chain from which the booth was hanging was locked in position. The booth began to descend.

"I suppose shouting 'help' wouldn't do any good?" Patsy shuddered.

They soon established that bashing the glass with their fists didn't do any good either. The concrete grew nearer and nearer.

"Rock!" shouted Jeremy suddenly.

"Not yet," said Patsy, "it's still liquid."

"No! Rock the booth!" Jeremy flung all his weight against one of the glass sides. Patsy realized what he was up to and joined in. Mustafa and Dontafa were still blindfolded, so all they could do was wonder what on earth was going on. The booth swung. Jeremy and Patsy leaped at the opposite side. It swung back. The swinging motion got wider and wider until –

Sss-KRRRRRAsssSHHHHH!

– it smashed against one of the machines. The prisoners tumbled to the floor in a shower of glass.

A loudly warbling alarm sounded. Agent Spanner covered his ears. "Oh, do we have to have that awful din every time something happens?"

Agent Wrench looked up from the computer console he was working at. His face twisted into something that would have given

Dracula nightmares. "Catch them!" he spat at a nearby mummy. "And keep the production line going!"

Over by the shattered booth, Jeremy and Patsy were undoing the ropes around Mustafa and Dontafa. The bodyguards flung off their blindfolds and blinked nervously as they took in their surroundings.

"Never doubted you for a minute, boys," lied Jeremy. "You try to find a way out, and alert anyone you can find. Patsy and I will fight off the mummies, shut down the factory, arrest Agent Wrench and Agent Spanner and ... er ... you know... On second thoughts, finding a way out is more a job for a highly trained secret agent..."

But the bodyguards had already hurried away into the darkness. Jeremy and Patsy went in the opposite direction, towards the huge, upside-down funnel-thing in the centre of the factory.

*　　*　　*

Agent Wrench checked pressure gauges and electronic read-outs, adjusted dials and operated switches. Agent Spanner was having a nice sit-down in the corner.

The noise of the machines rose. The conveyor belts moved faster. The central funnel shook, there was a loud KA-PING and a fully formed mummy dropped out with a crash. It stood up, its programming tuned it in to Jeremy and Patsy's location, and it moved off.

"Ha, ha, haaa, Haaa, HHaaaaaAAAAA Haaaa!" yelled Agent Wrench, among other things. He slapped his hands together with glee.

"Honestly, there's no need to get so excited," mumbled Agent Spanner.

The funnel began to tremble again. Another mummy appeared ...

KA-PING! Crash!

and another ...

KA-PING! Crash!

Chapter 6

In which there is a colossal explosion

....

Meanwhile, Jeremy and Patsy had quite enough mummies to contend with already. The mummies weren't nimble enough to catch them if they kept crawling underneath the conveyor belts, so they followed the line of the machines back towards the centre of the cavern.

"I thought Wrench and Spanner were MI7 agents!" said Patsy.

"They are," said Jeremy. "Or rather they were. I've got a feeling they may get the sack for this!"

"But what do they want an army of robots for?"

"Oh, come on, Patsy, what would you do with an army of robots?"

"Ummm," pondered Patsy, "force the Headmaster to ban double Geography."

"Exactly," said Jeremy. "They could do whatever they want. Take over Egypt, MI7, anything. And if anyone moves against them, they just churn out more robots."

"Sounds like fun," said Patsy.

"Patsy!" cried Jeremy, shocked. "It's an appalling way to behave, and you know it! They're no better than playground bullies."

Suddenly, a bandaged arm swung out and grabbed Patsy's ankle. She twisted round and kicked with her other foot. Her boot clanged hard against the robot's ear. Its head bent inwards, sparks flew and the mechanism holding her ankle let go enough for her to pull free.

"Looks like they've learned to crawl!" said Jeremy. They rolled out from under the conveyor belt and jumped to their feet.

Agent Wrench and Agent Spanner blocked their way forward. Mummies blocked their retreat.

"Don't have to go just yet, do you?" said Agent Wrench, creepily. "We've hardly begun to make your lives a misery."

"You really are being a dreadful nuisance," added Agent Spanner.

Jeremy pulled himself up to his full height, which was about half Agent Wrench's. "You, sir, are a disgrace to the Secret Service. And so is your trained monkey here."

Agent Spanner fought back the tears. "I say we get really, really horrid with them," he quivered. "Straight away."

"Do you honestly think that disposing of us will stop you being found out?" said Jeremy. "MI7 will simply send in more agents."

Agent Wrench flung out his arms, grinning madly at the machines all around them. "By then it will be too late. Spanner's genius for electronics, and my genius for dastardly plots of international proportions, have created the ultimate weapon. Out here in Egypt, apparently on a mission, we can keep away from prying eyes while we build our factory. With the so-called curse of Psidesalad II to terrify and confuse everyone, we can test our robots in the field. We are ready for anything. Let MI7 send a hundred agents! We'll nobble the lot of them!"

"You're barmy," said Patsy.

"And you, Ginger, are history," sneered Agent Wrench. He turned to the mummies. "Attack!"

The phrase "all hell broke loose" is one which should be used carefully. In a case like this, it would imply that a lot of bangs, crunches and other destructive noises were going on. It would also imply that things were thrown, shins were kicked, and evil villains were wrestled to the ground by the best friends of secret agents. And that's exactly what did happen, so...

All hell broke loose. Jeremy dodged the fists of two advancing mummies. They ploughed into a machine, making mummy-shaped dents in it. Jeremy dashed over to Agent Wrench's computer console.

"Hold them off, Patsy. I'll try to shut down the production line!"

*   *   *

A gang of mummies was hanging on to various parts of Patsy, so it was more a question of them holding her off. She had Agent Wrench's collar gripped tightly in one hand and Agent Spanner's in the other, so at least they were in a tight spot, too.

"Gerrof," spluttered Agent Wrench, turning blue.

"That's not very nice, now, is it?" gasped Agent Spanner, turning purple.

Jeremy's hands fluttered over the banks of controls in front of him. He thought hard about the MI7 "Stay Cool in a Crisis" lecture he'd been to. He examined the read-outs. He checked the dials. He made a calm, rational judgement about what codes he needed to tap into the computer to shut the production line off, and pressed the ENTER key. The production line speeded up.

Mummies started dropping out of the funnel at an alarming rate. They were coming at him from all directions, homing in on the intruder. Their arms reached out.

The conveyor belt next to Patsy was whizzing along now. Agent Wrench struggled wildly.

"Too fast!" he croaked. "It'll overload!"

With a whopping great SMACK, the conveyor belt buckled and snapped. One end whipped round and slapped a line of mummies into the air. The other end did the same to Patsy. Her scream as she was hurled upwards, clutching her bottom, is unrepeatable. She landed on top of the giant funnel, slipped, and only stopped herself falling by hanging on to the thick tubes which fed into the funnel's top. Several of them were split open, and jets of steam hissed in her face.

Jeremy watched helplessly. One mummy had both his arms, and another had both his legs. Luckily, all four limbs were still attached to his body. He'd worked out where he'd gone wrong at the controls, but there was no hope of having a second go. Agent Wrench and Agent Spanner were already hurrying over to the computer console and making the adjustments needed to stop the machines overloading.

Patsy got another blast of hot steam up her nose, and pulled out her hanky as a sneeze welled up. However, she'd forgotten that her hanky was still covered in the yucky mess Deidre had coated her with during their flight in the helicopter.

"*UUUrrrGGGHHggHH!*" she cried, understandably.

Jeremy twisted towards her as best he could. "Patsy! Stick it in the funnel!"

Only too glad to get rid of it, Patsy stuffed the dripping hanky into one of the split tubes she was hanging on to. A sharp, blue crackle of power suddenly lit the tube from inside. She let go and dropped to the floor.

Agent Wrench and Agent Spanner stopped what they were doing. "NoOOooo!" yelled

Agent Wrench. "You'll set the whole thing off! That slime will blow every circuit in it! My factory! My beautiful machines! My lovely world domination suit!"

The machines shook and split. One by one, in a chain reaction, they exploded.

WHUMPPPHHH!

Ka-WHhhhoOOOM!

PHHoOOWWWW!

The group of thirty-two tourists on a package tour organized by Sun & Sand Holidays Ltd were at that moment enjoying an open-air lunch by the pyramids. They hadn't got over having their tour ruined by a helicopter sandstorm in Chapter Four, but the company had persuaded them not to prosecute anyone. Their tour bus was parked nearby, ready to take them back to their hotel. The Sun & Sand representative was speaking to them slowly and calmly:

"So here we are, before we depart for rest and relaxation by the hotel pool, enjoying a traditional meal cooked specially by a team of local chefs. On your left, freshly baked loaves of bread. On your right, many dishes made to ancient recipes and ..." (a puzzled pause) "a colossal explosion?"

The tourists turned, curious. Sure enough, the top had blown off the nearest pyramid and was shooting up into the sky. A deafening series of bangs sent a gigantic ball of smoke and fire billowing into the air, and blown out ahead of it all were four figures.

The tourists watched as the figures flew in a neat arc, up, over the desert and down on top of their lunch. Jeremy and Patsy, their clothes and faces singed and smoking, crashed to an almost soft landing on the pile of bread. Agent Wrench and Agent Spanner skidded along the table, splattering food all over the tourists and into the waiting arms of Mustafa, Dontafa and the police.

Then the top of the pyramid arrived. By now, of course, it had crumbled into a couple of dozen huge, heavy blocks, and the falling blocks smashed what was left of the tourists' lunch, tour bus and nerves. Mrs Bedsit (from Hull) screamed at the top of her voice. Mr Bungalow (from Leamington Spa) was knocked unconscious by a flying lump of stone. The Sun & Sand rep wet himself.

Jeremy dusted himself down. "Another job successfully concluded, Patsy," he said proudly. "The robots around the city should have switched off too, now their control system is gone."

They wandered out across the sand, paying no attention to the wailing of the tourists, the pile of rubble surrounding the tourists or the dollops of hot food covering the tourists. Agent Wrench and Agent Spanner were already under arrest in a police car halfway to the airport.

"You know," said Jeremy, "when I write this up in my memoirs, I think I'll call the chapter 'How I Saved the World From Robot Domination, Single-Handed'."

Patsy, who'd had quite enough that day, spent a happy few minutes burying him upside down in the sand. But there was no time for mucking about. A beeping sound was coming from Jeremy's tie...

JEREMY BROWN
ON MARS

Chapter 1

In which Jeremy and Patsy travel several million miles

....

Grotside School, Thursday morning, about half past ten. Jeremy Brown, his best friend, Patsy Spudd, and the rest of the class were enduring the horrors of French with Madame Croissant. Unfortunately, Madame Croissant was quite capable of being horrible with or without French.

"Attention la classe!" she squeaked from under her tight bun of hair, which always looked like it was nailed to her head. *"Et maintenant, nous alons etudier la leçon numero douze!"*

"How are we ever going to know what foreign words mean if she only ever talks to us in foreign?" muttered Patsy under her breath.

Jeremy shrugged his shoulders. He was busy thinking about his last case. The rest of the class thought of him as that weedy-looking kid with glasses, but the glasses and scruffy appearance were simply a disguise. An exceptionally brilliant disguise, too, he always thought, because nobody had the slightest idea he was an undercover agent for MI7. Nobody except Patsy, that is, and he sometimes wished she was in the dark too, because she kept whispering things like:

"When are we off on another mission, then?"

"Shh!" said Jeremy. Madame Croissant was mercilessly brandishing irregular verbs. Anyone could fall prey to a grammar question at any moment.

"We haven't been called up since we solved the case of the Albanian ambassador's hollow legs," said Patsy.

"A fabulously clever piece of detective work on my part," said Jeremy, proudly. "Who would have guessed that they were being worked on strings by his dog?"

"It was me who blew the kneecaps off," said Patsy.

Madame Croissant slapped her hands together loudly. *"Ne parles pas en classe, Mademoiselle Pomme de Terre!"* she cried.

"Eh?" said Patsy.

"I wish we had another case," sighed Jeremy.

He'd regret having said that, because soon they would both be chased through an alien fortress by creatures with twenty-four tentacles each. If the full horror of this fate is to be revealed, the scene must first shift back a few hours in time, to the previous night…

The British University for Monitoring Stars (which only very silly people ever called BUMS) stood tall, dark and silent. In the woods behind it, an owl hooted sleepily.

There were no lights to be seen at any of the building's windows. The only light at all came from the soft glow of the moon and the stars, and from the blinking of tiny bulbs on high-tech scientific equipment in the university's many laboratories. Everyone had gone home.

Except for one person. A shadowy figure was moving slowly along the main corridor on the fifth floor. The figure wore soft shoes, made no sound and carried a large black bag.

Silently, the bag was placed on the floor. Its zip was pulled back with great care. From inside was lifted a sleek, metallic device, about the size and shape of a laptop PC. It was set down next to the bag. Small grippers suddenly sprang out from around its base and dug hard into the floor. Upwards from the top of the device whirred an antenna, at the tip of which flashed a tiny red light.

The stillness of the night was broken as the device began to emit a regular *bip-bip-bip-bip* as it transmitted a homing signal. The figure gathered up the bag, moved swiftly to the lifts and within minutes was out of the building and hurrying away. Up on the fifth floor, the homing beacon did its work.

The skies above the university gradually filled with a weird humming sound that rose and fell in a particularly creepy way. Luckily, nobody was around to witness the scene, because while the humming had been creepy, the strange way the stars now appeared to be wobbling would have made any witnesses rush home to change their trousers.

Suddenly, there was a flash. A wide red beam of energy shot vertically out of the sky and slammed into the roof of the building, on a direct line to the position of the beacon inside. With a whopping great WHOMPPPHH every window shattered.

A second red lightning bolt hit the same position. The university's walls shuddered, tottered and fell to bits in a rumbling tumble of concrete and dust. The wreckage settled into a giant heap, surrounded by swirls of what had recently been stairways and floors.

Slowly, with demolition complete, silence

and darkness returned. The skies were peaceful and the moon shone gently down on the rubble as if nothing out of the ordinary had happened.

"Nothing out of the ordinary has been happening," sighed Jeremy. "That's the trouble. Oo! Ow!"

That "Oo! Ow!" was caused by the sharp buzzing sensation he suddenly felt in his shoes. Since his shoes were where his secret MI7 communicator was hidden that day, his razor-sharp brain deduced that MI7 was trying to contact him. Either that or his feet had instantly grown eight sizes bigger, but he hadn't had that trouble since the case of the mutant Norwegians.

"Oo! Ow!" he winced again.

"*Vous avez un question, Monsieur Lebrun?*" squeaked Madame Croissant.

"No, Madame Croissant, I need to be excused. Er, lameness. It's hereditary. If I don't get medical attention immediately my feet swell and this horrible runny stuff comes out." He sprang up and hopped painfully to the door.

"Non! Non! Non!" squealed Madame Croissant, rapping her ruler on the edge of her desk. *"En français! En français!"*

"Oh," said Jeremy. *"Er, je voudrais … umm, aller au…* Oh, look, I really haven't got time for this, dreadfully sorry."

He hobbled out, followed by an icy stare from Madame Croissant and a wave of cruel laughter from the rest of the class (except from Patsy, of course, who realized exactly what was going on).

"Oo! Ow!"

Outside, in the chalky corridor, Jeremy quickly checked that nobody could see him. He pulled off his shoes, held the heel of the left one up to his ear and the heel of the right one up to his mouth.

"The blancmange is yellow," said the deep voice of his boss at MI7.

"Banana and pineapple flavoured,"

responded Jeremy correctly. "Morning, boss."

"Good morning, Agent Brown. Pay attention. Late last night, something caused the total destruction of the British University for Monitoring Stars."

"What (smirk), you mean (snigger) BUMS?" chortled Jeremy.

"Only very silly people call it BUMS," snapped his boss. "A strange force reduced it to rubble in a matter of seconds."

"What sort of strange force?" said Jeremy nervously, getting the feeling that it would turn out to be horribly dangerous.

"Evidence suggests a high energy beam fired from beyond Earth's atmosphere."

"Ah," said Jeremy, now absolutely sure that it was horribly dangerous. "Well, I'd love to help out, of course, but, umm, wouldn't this be best handled by an agent with more, you know, outer space experience?"

"We contacted all our agents with outer space experience," said his boss. "And now they're hiding under a table and won't come out. You're the only one left. Besides, the university is close to the school, so it'll save on travelling. Your mission is to discover the source of this energy beam and put it out of action. Operation Exit will be put into effect, as usual. That is all."

The bell went for the end of *la leçon*. The corridor was filled with clumping boots and flying textbooks. Jeremy put on his shoes, took off his glasses, smartened his tie and adopted his special secret agent cool look, which it had taken him ages to get right in the bathroom mirror at home.

Patsy didn't do anything to tidy herself up, because she preferred it that way. Her ginger hair looked like even a rat wouldn't have nested in it. "Are we off?" she said, excitedly.

"We're off," announced Jeremy. "They said the case was horribly dangerous, but I insisted on taking it anyway. First stop, the British University for Monitoring Stars."

"What, BUMS?" spluttered Patsy.

"Only very silly people call it BUMS," said Jeremy loftily.

Operation Exit, meanwhile, involved MI7 telephoning the Headmaster of Grotside School. He was told that he should sign letters allowing Jeremy and Patsy to be out of lessons for as long as they wanted, otherwise the world would get to hear about his subscription to *Fairytime Stories Monthly*.

Jeremy and Patsy collected their letters from his trembling hands on the way out of the school gates. They hurried off in the direction of what was left of the university.

What was left of the university was being clambered over by the people who, until the day before, had worked in it. They were salvaging what they could of the experiments they had been conducting, and the records they had kept, but all they were ending up with was a pile of shredded papers and battered equipment.

Jeremy and Patsy questioned one of the salvage team, and were directed to a tall man with a beard who was wearing a sagging knitted cardigan and an expression of intense rage. The cardigan and the expression were an identical shade of mauve. This was the Head of Research, Professor Killjoy.

"Good morning," said Jeremy politely, being careful not to get concrete dust on his trousers. "I am Jeremy Brown of the Secret Service, and this is my Field Tactics Manager, Patsy Spudd."

"Vandalism!" shouted the Professor. "Barbarism!"

"Oh dear," sniggered Patsy, looking around, "someone's exploded your BUMS. It's (smirk, giggle) a bit of a cheek, really. Ha, haaaa!"

"Patsy, pack it in," said Jeremy crossly.

"You can both pack it in!" shouted the Professor. "I don't need smarmy know-alls like you to tell me it was those hooligans from Grotside School over there that did it! Arrest the lot of them! Now!"

A smoothly calm female voice floated over the rubble. "Is that really a credible theory, Professor?"

The elegant Dr Nicely appeared. Their surroundings were tattered, devastated and ugly: Dr Nicely was the exact opposite. She held out a slender hand to Jeremy as she introduced herself.

"Do call me Heather," she purred, with a smile. Jeremy just grinned soppily and mumbled something about being delighted. Patsy made throwing-up noises. "The Professor is letting his emotions run away with him," said Dr Nicely. "This is the result of a directed high energy beam."

Dr Nicely was accompanied by her lab assistant, Wallingford Horatio Smith. Their surroundings were grubby, greasy and grey: Mr Smith was exactly the same. He scribbled notes on his clipboard.

"Do call me Mr Smith," he droned icily. "My colleagues are both wrong. This is due to freak earthquake activity."

"Balderdash!" shouted the Professor. "Twaddle!"

The three of them started up a heated debate on the causes of concrete crumbling and the exact nature of balderdash. Jeremy and Patsy looked at each other helplessly.

"Fat lot of use this bunch are going to be," said Patsy. "Still, at least they're not taking it sitting down. Ha, haaaa! Can't be much fun having an energy beam right up their—"

"I do hope, Mr Brown," purred Dr Nicely, "that your friend won't be referring to the university as—"

"Good heavens no!" said Jeremy quickly, blushing. "Only very silly people do that. Come along, Patsy, we must, er … search something."

"You could start in the woods over there," said Dr Nicely. "It would be an ideal place to hide the kind of very large mechanism needed to fire an energy beam of such power."

"What a perfectly perfect idea," said Jeremy, blushing again. "Do excuse us." He hurried Patsy away before she could say anything embarrassing.

They didn't find any large mechanisms in the woods. What they found was a door.

"At least, I think it's a door," said Jeremy.

It was tall, round and silvery, standing upright and on its own in a small clearing. Jeremy ran a hand across its surface. His voice went slightly spooky. "You know, Patsy, I get the impression that this thing isn't from Earth at all. It looks metal, but it feels sort of like plastic. It's warm, as if it's powered up. And there are symbols pressed into it, all over. Look closely. That's not any language I've ever seen."

"Well, it's not French," mumbled Patsy.

Jeremy's fingers strayed across a rectangular panel in the middle of the door. It suddenly hummed loudly and the door slid back, revealing a swirling, greeny-grey vortex of light.

"Uh-oh!" said Jeremy.

"Hey, brilliant!" said Patsy. "Let's go through!"

If he'd had time, Jeremy would have given stern warnings about the dangers of jumping into sinister, extraterrestrial vortexes. As it was, Patsy bounded in, dragging Jeremy after her. The vortex instantly transported them several million miles.

The door hummed shut.

Chapter 2

In which beings from a distant world issue a very large bill

....

The room into which Jeremy and Patsy stepped was very long, very low and very white. The transport portal door behind them clicked and deactivated as it closed.

"Crumbs," whispered Jeremy.

"Fantastic!" cried Patsy. The word bounced off the walls and wrapped itself back around their ears a few times. "Where are we?"

Their footsteps made echoey clacking noises as they walked forward slowly. Jeremy approached a wide rectangle set deep into one of the walls. Delicately, he reached out to the smaller rectangular panel at its centre. "I expect this opens the same way as that door," he said. "Logic suggests that it ought to be the shutter for a window."

And so it was. As his fingers touched the

panel, the whole thing slid upwards with a sharp hiss. Through the thick plexiglass was a vast landscape of dusty red plains and mountains, topped with a cloudless, pinky-purple sky.

"Good grief," whispered Jeremy, eyes wide.

"WwwoooooWW!" cried Patsy, squashing her face against the window and steaming it up with her breath. "It's another planet! It's a real life another planet! It's—"

"Mars," whispered Jeremy.

"WwwoooooWW!" cried Patsy again. "Time to explore!"

Jeremy looked back at the transport portal through which they had travelled. "Well, we know what's back that way," he said. "Let's see now…"

He wandered over to the far wall, which had an even bigger rectangle set into it. This one covered almost the entire end of the room, and reached from floor to ceiling. Once again, there was a smaller rectangular panel at its centre.

"Logic suggests that this ought to be a door," said Jeremy. "You know, it's lucky there's someone as clever as me around to work these things out. Did I ever tell you about the time I unlocked a safe during a six hundred metre plunge into a vat of blue paint?"

"Far too often," mumbled Patsy.

"I just hope we don't encounter any terrifying alien nasties," said Jeremy.

He reached out and pressed the opening panel. Up hissed the door. Beyond it was an enormous control room, packed with weird machines, read-out screens …

and terrifying alien nasties!

They looked at Jeremy and Patsy.

Jeremy and Patsy looked at them.

"Run!" yelled Patsy.

They made a dash for a long corridor which snaked away from the control room. All together, the aliens let out a spine-chilling, wailing screech and gave chase.

Patsy was in the lead, her stout boots ideal

for running-away-type situations. Jeremy glanced over his shoulder. There were dozens of creatures right behind them, each with a stumpy round body, three eyes waving about on thick stalks and twenty-four shivering tentacles which served as both arms and legs. They also smelled of cheese. Jeremy thought they were utterly hideous and completely frightening. (The aliens thought Jeremy was utterly hideous too, with his one nose and his four, jointed stick things. Unfortunately, *he* didn't frighten *them* one little bit.)

"Bok phaan parr'chak xa!" howled the one closest to snagging him with a flying tentacle. Then the creature realized it hadn't got its translator strapped on. It slipped a flat, grille-like device over its slit-like mouth and tried again. "Earthlings will halt! Earthlings are in violation of Rule 913, Paragraph 8, Subsection 2 of the Law of Pursuit! Earthlings will halt!"

"Hurry!" yelled Jeremy.

A loud, warbling intruder alarm started up.

All the other aliens strapped on their translators and issued information about the penalties for breaking the law.

Jeremy's and Patsy's energy was beginning to sag. Jeremy made a mental note to eat a more nutritious breakfast in future. The smell of cheese was making Patsy feel peckish.

They were running through an immense docking bay. Small, oval-shaped space vehicles were loaded into long, see-through tubes. The doors to the tubes were hanging open on chunky hinges.

"Escape capsules!" cried Jeremy, exhausted. "Patsy! Inside!"

"We can't fly one of them!" gasped Patsy.

"We can't escape this lot, either!" cried Jeremy.

Patsy dived through the miniature airlock of the nearest capsule. Jeremy scrambled in after her. Quickly, they slammed the door shut behind them. Its thick locking clamps automatically *ka-chunk*ed into place.

In seconds, dozens of tentacles were slapping angrily against it.

Jeremy and Patsy wriggled uncomfortably in the cramped interior of the capsule. There was barely room for the two of them, and what room there was had been designed to seat creatures with wriggly things for legs. Aliens crowded around the launch tube, peering in at them, their eyes twisting around for a better look.

"Press something!" said Patsy. "Get us out of here!"

Detecting their presence, the capsule's command system suddenly came on, lighting up the flight control panels. "Translation mode on," it said, peacefully. "Thank you for choosing Escape-o-Pod. Fee for use will be two hundred credits, payable at the end of your flight."

Jeremy slapped his fist on the big red button marked LAUNCH.

"Oh, goody, something to eat," said Patsy.

"Launch," tutted Jeremy, "not lunch."

In an instant, they were squashed to the back of the capsule as it fired like a bullet up the launch tube and out into the Martian atmosphere. Suddenly, there was wide open space all around. Their stomachs did a couple of somersaults, decided that was a bad idea and shrunk down towards their feet instead.

"Yeeeehaaaa!" cried Patsy.

"I don't feel well," cried Jeremy.

About a dozen other capsules were being launched right behind them. The aliens at the controls had been specially trained for space combat, and had each spent hundreds of credits learning to fly their machines.

Jeremy and Patsy hadn't.

"They're gaining on us!" said Patsy, watching the large tactical display which had blinked into life next to her left ear.

"They wouldn't be chasing us if they couldn't bring us down," reasoned Jeremy. "They're probably armed."

Glowing, round energy bolts exploded

against the outside of the capsule. It rocked and dipped wildly. More bolts flew past them, scorching the capsule's casing and windows.

"Why do I always have to be right?" Jeremy wailed. Then he turned to the flight controls. "Command system, do you understand me?"

"Translation mode on," said the command system, even more peacefully than before.

"Evasive manoeuvres!" said Jeremy.

"Optional evasive manoeuvres program is available at an additional charge of five hundred credits."

"Do it!" said Jeremy. "And switch on whatever ray guns we've got!"

"Thank you," said the command system. "U-Blast-'Em torpedoes supplied at forty-five credits per unit."

A bulky pair of joysticks hummed into view next to Patsy, alongside a display showing targeting information. She flipped the safety cover off the FIRE button.

"Cool." She grinned.

The capsule ducked and dived as the evasive manoeuvres program switched itself on. Jeremy and Patsy were squashed from one side to another and back again. Through the windows, the red mountains of Mars seemed to whirl and twist ahead of them.

Patsy let rip with a volley of torpedoes every time one of their pursuers came in range. She didn't actually hit anything, but she had loads of fun trying.

The aliens' capsules buzzed and whizzed. Their much more carefully aimed shots were rapidly destroying the outer casing of Jeremy and Patsy's craft. Warning lights kept coming on all over the flight controls.

"Vital systems damaged," said the command system as peacefully as it was possible to say it. "Destruction likely. Thank you for your custom."

"We've got to get back to the alien base or we'll be blown to bits," said Jeremy.

"Oh, let's take one of these capsules, Patsy, he says," grumbled Patsy. "Let's escape, he says. Thanks a heap! I get tested on French grammar *and* blown to bits on the same day!"

Jeremy ignored her. "Got to think of a way to get us back," he muttered.

The capsule shook violently as another barrage of bolts pounded it. Parts of the engine vaporized, and showers of hull fragments exploded all over the place. Then the capsule spun rapidly as a small hole was blasted in its main window. Air began to rush out.

The evasive manoeuvres program decided the situation was hopeless, and erased itself. Now the capsule was hurtling along in a straight line which would take it out into the depths of space.

Jeremy reckoned his brain had erased itself too.

"Wait," said Patsy. "I know a way to turn the capsule around and return to the alien base!"

"Patsy, you're a marvel!" cried Jeremy.

"Have you worked out a way to bypass the flight control systems?"

"No, we just press this button here marked RETURN TO BASE."

She pressed it.

The capsule whirled upwards, round and back the way it had come, at a speed which left Jeremy and Patsy trying very hard not to think of greasy food. The pursuing aliens didn't have time to react before it was out of their firing range.

As they neared the alien base, Jeremy noticed something which would turn out to be important when they reached Chapter Three.

The capsule shot back down its launch tube, and into the loading bay. It skidded to a halt at the end of the corridor along which our heroes had been chased, and steamed quietly to itself.

"Total bill for usage and repairs is one hundred and thirty-four thousand, two hundred and forty-one credits," coughed the command system weakly. "Please place payment in the slot marked PAYMENT. Any recognized galactic currency is acceptable. We look forward to your next escape flight with us."

"What?" cried Patsy. "We haven't got any recognized galactic currency!"

Jeremy pulled his French exercise book from his pocket, ripped out the pages, and stuffed them into the slot. The capsule's accounting system had been badly damaged, and mistook them for Plutonian dollars. The door's locking clamps unhooked themselves with a hiss.

Jeremy and Patsy kicked open the door and tumbled out. Aliens were already appearing from the other end of the docking bay, rippling towards them on their tentacles. Without a word, Patsy hauled Jeremy to his feet and they ran back down the corridor as fast as their shaky legs and even shakier stomachs would take them.

The corridor was clear, but the control

room was back to being fully manned. Well, fully aliened. The aliens all turned at the same time and, adjusting their translators, hurried forward to intercept.

"Earthlings are prohibited by Order 563, Article B!"

"Failure to comply will result in a term of imprisonment!"

"Failure to halt is not in line with accepted procedure!"

They rushed at them, eye-stalks and tentacles waving.

"Hurry!" called Patsy. Jeremy quickly placed his hand on the door of the transport portal. As soon as it was open wide enough to step through, Patsy pushed him into the vortex.

"See ya!" she called to the aliens, jumping in herself as tentacles swung out to grab her legs. The door hummed shut.

Chapter 3

In which Earth's defences are neutralized and Patsy gets really, really hungry

···

The woods were reassuringly full of twittering birds and burrowing moles. Frankly, Jeremy and Patsy wouldn't have cared if the moles had been twittering and the birds burrowing, they were just glad to be back on a familiar planet. They glanced at the closed portal behind them. It stayed shut.

"I don't think they're going to follow us," gasped Jeremy, trying to catch his breath. They set off wearily, out of the woods.

"Maybe they can't survive in our atmosphere?" said Patsy.

"No, we were OK on their base, remember. They breathe air like we do. Which means they're not from Mars, because Mars doesn't have an atmosphere like ours." Jeremy combed his hair while he thought about the situation. "I don't think they want to be seen on Earth. Not yet."

"Why?" said Patsy.

"Well, look at them. They'd have real trouble trying to dress up as humans and blend in. They're keeping their distance until their plans are more advanced."

"So how did this transporter door thing get here?"

"Elementary, my dear Patsy," said Jeremy. "They're being helped."

If the two of them had been characters in a movie, this would have been the perfect point for a *dan-dan-daaaa* bit. But they weren't. So it wasn't. Instead, Jeremy made another observation, based on his reading of the MI7 booklet "Dangerous Gadgets at a Glance".

"When we were in the escape capsule, on the way back to the base, did you notice something?" (This is the something from page 192.)

"What sort of something?" said Patsy.

"A sort of enormous cannon-type something that could easily have been the device used to fire the energy beam which destroyed the university?"

"No, I didn't," said Patsy.

"Lucky I did, then," said Jeremy. "And if the beam was fired from Mars, I bet it needed a homing beacon to reach its target accurately. Which means somebody placed one."

"Which confirms they're being helped," concluded Patsy.

"Hmm," said Jeremy. "The plot is thickening faster than school gravy."

He was right. The aliens, on their Martian base, had done three important things:

1) Cleaned up the mess left by Jeremy and Patsy.

2) Brought forward their attack plans, because Jeremy and Patsy had found their base and would now try to foil their evil schemes.

3) Put on their blue combat shirts. These combat shirts were covered in disgustingly

rude insults, written in twenty-seven galactic languages so that the aliens could be nasty to as many beings as possible all in one go.

In the control room, the aliens' leader, distinguishable by the floppy Hat of Grandness he wore, settled into his squidgy throne behind his electronic campaign desk. This was Gruntox the Big. At his side stood his second in command, Dungsit the Many Tentacled. Their words are shown here in translation.

"As advised by Section B of the Destruction of Earth Act," grunted Gruntox, "move the scoopotron out of hiding place D and into Position 1!"

"Aye, aye, Your Bigness!" Dungsit saluted with four of his many tentacles.

"And don't muck it up, Dungsit!" grunted Gruntox.

"No, no, Your Bigness!"

Dungsit rippled over to a mobile control unit and wrapped tentacles around two fat levers which jutted out at the front. Above the levers was a screen, and on the screen could be seen the Earth, and the Moon...

On the dark side of the Moon, hidden well out of sight, the scoopotron floated gently in space. It was the size of six football pitches, but wasn't nearly as green, and out of one end unwound what looked like an immensely long, fat hose.

As Dungsit pushed and pulled levers back on Mars, the scoopotron's engines powered up. It glided gracefully out of the Moon's shadow, and headed down towards the surface of the Earth ... towards the northern hemisphere ... towards Europe...

In dozens of tracking stations, situated in dozens of countries, the scoopotron appeared as an enormous blip on radar screens which had, until now, always managed to stay free of menacing alien war machines. The people at these tracking stations weren't entirely sure what to do. First, they ran up and down and cried for their mums. Then, they had some sweeties and an ice cream, and that made them feel better. Finally, they launched every missile and fighter aircraft they had.

A wave of weaponry closed in on the alien invader...

"Wave of weaponry closing in!" called Gruntox's third in command, Podclone the Fat, from a console at the other end of the control room.

Gruntox turned to Dungsit. "Procedure 158, Amendment 2!" he growled.

"Aye, aye, Your Bigness!" saluted Dungsit. He pulled more levers.

"And make sure you pull the right ones, Dungsit!" growled Gruntox.

"Aye, aye, Your Bigness!"

"Wave of weaponry neutralized!" called Podclone a few moments later. "Offensive material has been pushed back to ground level! Cost of attack holding steady at two million credits!"

Gruntox grinned horribly to himself. How he loved pulverizing little planets, and how he loved doing it without having to spend a fortune. "Soon it will be ours," he dribbled. "All of it. Billions and trillions of credits' worth." He started giggling sneakily behind a couple of tentacles.

All the other aliens in the control room started giggling too. Gruntox's fourth in command, Mary the Stupidly Named, pulled himself together enough to make his report. "Our Earth agent has completed form T216, Your Bigness, to inform you that the next homing beacon will soon be in place, at Target 2…"

At Grotside School, the bell rang for lunchtime. It didn't ring for long, of course, because it liked to be nice and quiet by the time pupils started thundering past, otherwise it'd be smacked with a hockey stick.

The corridors and stairways were suddenly

crammed with people rushing in opposite directions. The more daring and reckless pupils were heading for the Dining Hall. The more sensible and health-conscious ones were steering well clear of the Dining Hall, and heading off home or into town for lunch. The teachers were making a dash for the Staff Room, where they could sit in thick tobacco smoke, drink coffee and try to steady their trembling nerves ready for the afternoon.

Amid the confusion and the clouds of chalk dust, a mysterious figure walked almost unnoticed. The figure carried a black bag. To one side of the school's entrance hall, which was slap bang in the middle of the main building, the figure stopped, crouched and unzipped the bag.

From inside was lifted a sleek, metallic device. The figure held it delicately against the nearest wall. Small grippers suddenly sprang out from around its base and dug hard into the concrete. An antenna whirred upwards from its top, and at the tip of the antenna flashed a tiny red light. The homing beacon began to emit a regular *bip-bip-bip-bip* as the figure hurried away...

Meanwhile, Jeremy was coming to a conclusion.

"...So in conclusion," he said, "I reckon that the aliens' agent on Earth is likely to be someone from the university itself. It would be an ideal first target, you see, because the agent wouldn't have to get into some strange building, where any number of alarms might be set off."

Patsy was humming quietly to herself, with her fingers in her ears. Jeremy hadn't noticed.

"Which means," he continued, "that the aliens weren't trying to destroy the university as such. They just wanted to destroy ... something convenient. Which also means that – Patsy, are you listening?"

"No."

Jeremy sulked all the way back to the

enormous pile of rubble that had once been the university. Professor Killjoy, Dr Nicely and Mr Smith were sitting on crumpled bits of filing cabinet, tucking into a posh-looking hamper of food.

"Splendid!" shouted the Professor, gobbling down half a pork pie. "Excellent!"

Dr Nicely waved at Jeremy, and he blushed yet again. "Do join us," she said. "Just something I threw together from a few leftovers at home. Salad with vinegar dressing, mushroom and kiwi fruit vol au vents, lobster with spicy Mexican salsa dip…"

"Got any chips?" said Patsy.

Jeremy perched next to Dr Nicely and picked up a slice of broccoli quiche, which he held with his little finger sticking out. "Thanks ever so much," he said with a soppy grin.

Mr Smith nibbled at a water biscuit. Patsy pulled a face at the taste of the spicy Mexican salsa dip.

"Are your investigations progressing, Mr Brown?" said Dr Nicely.

"We've made some significant discoveries, Dr Nicely, thank you for asking," said Jeremy. "Although they are, I'm afraid, of a rather disturbing and terrifying nature."

"We're gonna be got by aliens," spluttered Patsy through a mouthful of garlic sausage. She pulled another face and spat the sausage out into a paper napkin.

"Aliens!" shouted the Professor. "Rubbish!"

"The existence of life in other parts of the galaxy has yet to be proved," said Mr Smith.

"I'm sure we wouldn't be lied to by someone of Mr Brown's standing," said Dr Nicely. "Or his friend."

"I'm not listening to some lah-de-dah MI7 twaddle!" shouted the Professor.

"You never know, perhaps the aliens are in league with the Loch Ness Monster," said Mr Smith dryly, pushing his tiny round glasses back up to the top of his nose.

"I'm afraid I must tell you that they *are* in league with someone on Earth," said Jeremy, trying to sound dramatic and exciting, and yet at the same time confident and reassuring. He did quite a good job of it, actually.

"Yeah, it's one of you lot," said Patsy. She bit into an onion flan, pulled another face, and flung the rest of the flan over her shoulder.

"One of us?" yelled the Professor. "Piffle!"

"Perhaps one of us *is* the Loch Ness Monster," droned Mr Smith.

"Are you quite sure?" said Dr Nicely. One of her neat eyebrows arched elegantly.

"Yes," said Jeremy, blushing all over again. "But don't worry. I'm on the case. I once saved a train by swallowing the miniature timer on a three tonne bomb."

"Then he puked it up out of the window," said Patsy.

"Thank you, Patsy," said Jeremy through gritted teeth. "Any other intellectual gems you'd like to add to the conversation?"

Patsy was now feeling really, really hungry. She nearly said, "Yes, let's go and get some chips before the shop shuts," but instead she pointed to an object she'd spotted in the sky. An object with a long hose-thing snaking out in front of it.

"What's that?" she cried.

"Ah!" shouted the Professor. "That'll be the men from the council, come to start clearing away all this rubble!"

The scoopotron descended at about the same speed as Jeremy's and Patsy's jaws. Its engines rose to a howling roar. The hose, its end the width of the Channel Tunnel, dipped towards the rubble. With a rumbling clatter, lumps of concrete began to be sucked up.

The humans crawled away as fast as they could manage. The suction pulled hard on their clothes and hair. The remains of the picnic splattered and bounced over the debris, and shot up into the machine with a slurp.

"They only had to send a lorry!" yelled the Professor.

"That's not from the council!" yelled Dr Nicely. "That's from another planet!"

The five humans scattered, gradually finding movement easier as they got further from the scoopotron. Jeremy and Patsy took cover behind a post box.

"They want the building itself!" cried Patsy.

"They must have brought their plans forward, letting that thing out in the open so soon!" cried Jeremy. "But if all it does is suck up concrete, it won't have much to keep itself occupied with. Unless there's about to be a second target!"

"Such as?"

"Don't know," muttered Jeremy thoughtfully. "Just here there's only the woods, and the university, and ... the school! Patsy, they're going to destroy the school!"

"Yippee!"

"Patsy! People could get hurt! The aliens'

agent must have planted a homing beacon somewhere in the school buildings. We've got to deactivate it before it's—"

Too late. A weird humming spread out across the area, even louder than the sound of the scoopotron. The air itself seemed to shake and blur. Helplessly, Jeremy and Patsy watched as a fat red beam of energy flashed vertically from the sky.

The school playing fields erupted, shooting mud and grass hundreds of metres in all directions. Violent tremors knocked Jeremy and Patsy off their feet.

"They're closing in!" Patsy cried.

Chapter 4

In which our heroes risk life and limb and get no thanks for it at all

"Thank goodness it's lunchtime," said Jeremy. "Half the buildings are empty."

A second energy beam flashed into the school swimming pool. The pool vaporized in a cloud of high-pressure steam.

"Quick!" cried Patsy. "We've got to find that beacon!"

They ran to the school, bent double as if ducking out of the way of something. It was a pointless thing to do, because nothing could have stopped them being disintegrated if a beam had actually hit them. But they did it anyway.

The weird humming sound was building up all around them again. Another blast was seconds away. They hurtled into the entrance hall of the main school building, and slid to a halt on the highly polished floor.

"Oi!" came a grumpy voice from behind them. "I just finished shining that!" Mr Vim, the school caretaker, bustled towards them. His black moustache was as bristly as his broom, and his brown overalls were dotted with old paint stains.

"There!" cried Patsy, spotting the beacon clamped to the wall. They hurried over to it.

"Thank goodness the aliens' agent has no imagination," said Jeremy. "Or we might never have found it." He set to work examining the device.

"Oi!" barked Mr Vim. "I said I just finished shining that floor! Look at the marks you've put on it!"

"I'm really sorry, Mr Vim," said Jeremy, "but the whole school's about to explode. Please excuse me." He searched around the beacon's casing for a control panel. At one end was a touch sensor. He pressed it and a little hatch flipped open, revealing a set of buttons with alien symbols on them.

"An hour and a half I spent doing that, you

young thug," grumbled Mr Vim. "I'm going to report you!"

Outside, the humming in the sky reached a note that the school choir had been searching for since Christmas. A red flash suddenly slammed into the far end of the Modern Languages block. Half the building instantly shattered with a deafening BANG.

Fortunately, the far end of the Modern Languages block hadn't contained a single pupil. Unfortunately, it *had* contained the Staff Room and the Headmaster's private study. As the building exploded, twenty-eight screaming teachers were shot high into the air. The smoke trails which followed them were partly their tobacco, partly their clothes on fire.

Fortunately, none of them sustained serious damage: seven (including Madame Croissant) landed in nearby trees; eleven made teacher-shaped holes in other buildings; eight were flipped onto the roof of the gym; one would have had a soft landing if the swimming pool had still contained water. The Headmaster was shot across the mess that had now replaced the playing fields and slithered to a stop in a muddy trench. The copy of *Fairytime Stories Monthly* he'd been happily reading in his study had burnt away to little crispy bits.

Jeremy was determined to deactivate the beacon using logical reasoning and the application of intelligent thought. He also had no idea where to begin.

"Let's just smash it!" cried Patsy. "The next shot could hit *us*!"

"Patsy," said Jeremy, "there's no need to resort to mindless violence."

"I'm going to get a mop and a bucket!" grumbled Mr Vim. "You can clean off those marks yourselves!"

The walls around them suddenly buckled and split. A thunderous rumble of dust and smoke billowed through the hall. Mr Vim, clutching his broom tightly, was blown out of the building like a cork from a bottle.

"So much for being sensible," wailed Jeremy. "Smash it!"

With one flying kick from Patsy, the beacon was in pieces.

And so was the main building. Another blast pulverized six classrooms and a toilet block.

"It's made no difference!" yelled Jeremy. "Their targeting systems must have a firm lock on the school. There's only one thing for it now, Patsy. We've got to go back to Mars and shut the whole thing down!"

"Oh, great," said Patsy. "Another chance to risk life and limb. Hurray."

"Patsy," said Jeremy grandly, "it is our duty and our privilege to fight evil, even if it means facing horrible dangers and getting all grubby. Now come on."

Ducking pieces of flying school and scrambling past mounds of classroom, they headed for the portal in the woods.

They kept well clear of the scoopotron, which was still busy sucking up lumps of concrete. Behind them, the humming noise was rising again.

They hurried along the muddy path between the trees and bushes.

"What's that vacuum machine thing doing?" said Patsy.

"The best person to tell us has to be the aliens' agent," said Jeremy.

"And the aliens' agent has to be Dr Nicely!"

"Don't be silly," said Jeremy, "she wouldn't hurt a fly, let alone betray her entire planet to a bunch of intergalactic tentacled monsters! It's clearly Professor Killjoy."

"Oh, yeah? Nicely knew it was an energy beam that had blown up the university! *And* she was the one who suggested searching these woods! *And* she pointed out that vacuum machine thing is alien!"

"She's simply a highly intelligent person,"

said Jeremy, blushing just ever so slightly. "Witty and refined. We have a lot in common. Besides, if it was her she'd try to throw us off the scent, not reveal things that are true. No, mark my words, Killjoy's the villain."

"Why?"

"He's a right misery, that's why."

They came to a sudden halt. The portal's door was already open. Through it they could see the swirling vortex that led to the aliens' Martian fortress.

"I think we're about to find out, one way or the other," said Jeremy. "Looks like their agent has just this minute gone through!"

Pausing only to give each other a quick "Oh, crumbs" look, they stepped into the vortex themselves.

In the Martian control room, Gruntox and the rest of the aliens were getting so excited they were beginning to wobble up and down in their seats.

"Concrete!" gurgled Gruntox, his tentacles wriggling. "Lovely concrete!"

"We love concrete!" chorused the other aliens. Then they giggled a bit.

A humanoid figure, their agent on Earth, watched them from the shadows, smiling an evil, greedy smile.

"Scoopotron now in position C12!" said Dungsit, pulling levers on the scoopotron's control unit. "Scoopotron belly now holding 567.9 mega-loads, Your Bigness!"

"Lovely, lovely," gurgled Gruntox. "Don't muck it up, Dungsit, steady as she goes."

"Aye, aye, sir!"

"Zap-o-Matic energy beam ready to fire again, Your Bigness!" called Podclone. Two of his tentacles were poised over the button that would launch another attack on the school.

"Wait!"

Jeremy's voice was as loud and commanding as he could make it. The aliens' eyes swivelled around on their stalks and glared at him. Jeremy had adopted a heroic, arms folded, legs apart stance (which he'd learned from volume three of the MI7 manual *Be Cool With Body Posture*) in order to show the aliens he meant business. Patsy just made rude signs at them.

"Humans are illegal!" grizzled Gruntox into his translator. "Interference is illegal! Seize them in accordance with the Grabbing of Prisoners Act!"

Half a dozen aliens slithered over and wrapped tentacles tightly around Jeremy's and Patsy's arms. They were dragged over to Gruntox's throne. Patsy struggled like mad.

"Don't fight them, Patsy," said Jeremy. "We're here to talk." He turned to Gruntox. Now he actually had a chance to speak to the aliens, he wasn't entirely sure what to say to them. "Look, just stop all this nonsense, OK?"

"Yeah, game over, Ugly," said Patsy.

Gruntox called up a string of symbols on his control screen. "These two humans are in violation of two hundred and twenty-six separate regulations. They have an unpaid escape pod bill, which they attempted to settle using forged Plutonian dollars! They will be held in prison until they hand over enough credits to pay for their trial!"

"Why not simply throw them outside?" said a cold, calm voice from the shadows. "They wouldn't last two minutes in the Martian atmosphere. Then we'd be rid of them."

"That would be the cheapest option, Your Bigness," called Podclone, tapping at a calculator.

Patsy screwed up her eyes in an effort to see who the aliens' agent was. She needn't have bothered, because at that moment the thin, grey figure of the lab assistant, Mr Smith, stepped forward into a pool of light beside Gruntox's throne.

"I *knew* it wasn't Dr Nicely," said Jeremy.

"I leave their fate in your tentacles, Your Bigness," said Mr Smith. "The invasion must continue. Give me more beacons and I'll return to Earth and prepare more targets."

"Why are you doing this, Smith?" said Jeremy. "And who are these aliens?"

Mr Smith pushed his little, round glasses back to the top of his nose. His flat, dull smile made even Gruntox shiver. "I made contact through my work at the university. I picked up a random subspace transmission, and answered it. Gruntox the Big and his business partners here roam the Galaxy in search of—"

"Concrete," gurgled Gruntox, "lovely concrete. Beeaaauuuuutiful."

"It's very rare and precious in many parts of space," said Mr Smith. "I led them to our unprofitable little planet, which of course is positively covered in it. I'm helping them take control of Earth."

"And in return," said Jeremy, "they're giving you loads of—"

"Money," gurgled Mr Smith, "lovely money. Beeaaauuuuutiful. Gruntox and I can't exactly wear each other's combat shirts, but we're still two of a kind."

Gruntox and the other aliens giggled behind their tentacles in a way which Patsy thought rather silly and childish. Mr Smith operated a set of controls by Gruntox's throne, and a huge bag full of homing beacons came up through a hatch in the floor. He heaved the bag onto his shoulder.

"Goodbye, Mr Brown. Goodbye, Miss Spudd. Why not start trade talks with the aliens? You never know, you might be able to sell them your garden patio for a few credits. Before they come and take it, ha, ha, ha, ha."

Jeremy had a sudden idea, and he often found that ideas which turned up suddenly were the best ones.

"Good!" he said loudly, so that the entire control room could hear him. "Can't wait to be rid of it. Full of concrete-worm, it is. Falling apart."

"Eh?" said Mr Smith.

Gruntox fumbled hurriedly with his

translator, to make sure it was working properly. "The human will repeat himself by order of Rule 55!"

"Of course!" cried Jeremy, even louder. "I said our concrete at home has got concrete-worm. Right through it. It's falling to bits."

Patsy caught on to what he was up to. She started giggling in a way which the aliens thought rather silly and childish. Gruntox came over all faint and dizzy.

"The human will explain concrete-worm!" he gibbered. "What does it do to l-l-lovely concrete?"

"Don't listen to him!" cried Mr Smith. "He's lying! He's jealous of our deal!"

"Concrete-worm, or *Nastius chewemupius* to give it its full name, is a tiny, burrowing insect," proclaimed Jeremy. "It lays little pink eggs in deep holes in any concrete structure. These eggs hatch, and the furry things with teeth that come out eat all the concrete around them."

The aliens shivered with disgust. Some of

them wrapped shaking tentacles around their mouths to stop themselves being sick.

"Ignore him!" screamed Mr Smith. "He's just trying to rob me of my money!"

"They're a constant problem," continued Jeremy. All the aliens gasped. "Humans spend billions of credits every year fumigating buildings and stuff…" Several aliens wet their combat shirts. "We humans have to keep painting over our concrete with washing-up liquid and milk to protect it…" The aliens that didn't squeal with horror ran straight for the toilets.

"Why didn't you warn us of this, Smith?" gargled Gruntox, trying not to cry.

"Because it's *not true!*" screeched Mr Smith, his face turning from grey to purple.

"Oh now, be fair, Mr Smith," said Jeremy. "You wanted these poor aliens' money. Of course you weren't going to tell them about concrete-worm." He turned to Gruntox. "That makes sense, doesn't it, Your Bigness?"

Gruntox nodded, stuffing a hanky into his mouth.

"We came here to put you in the picture, didn't we, Patsy?" said Jeremy. "I mean, Earthlings are fair and honest. We couldn't let you have contaminated concrete. Wouldn't be good for business."

"C-c-contaminated," gurgled Gruntox, sobbing.

Podclone tapped hurriedly at his calculator. "Costs of decontamination are ... are ... are beyond calculation, Your Bigness!" he wailed.

"Of course, there's galloping sand rot in most concrete too," added Jeremy.

Gruntox pulled himself together and stood up.

"Invasion is cancelled, in line with Emergency Planning Procedures! This base is to be recycled! Humans will be ejected!"

Chapter 5

In which the aliens stick to the rules and Jeremy sticks to the floor

....

"Ejected?" howled Mr Smith. "After all I've done for you?"

Podclone rippled over to Gruntox clutching a thick wad of papers, and whispered something while pointing to a tiny, printed footnote on the last sheet. Gruntox nodded, and turned to Mr Smith.

"Not ejected, Smith," he growled. Mr Smith gasped with relief. "Sold!" grunted Gruntox. Mr Smith gasped with horror.

"What?" he yelled.

"Paragraph 9, Subsection 34, Condition 12 of your contract clearly states that your body and all its contents become our property if invasion plans are called off at any time for any reason in any way! Those are the rules! You will work for twenty years in the Invoicing Department on Andromeda –

without pay! Take him away!"

Mr Smith turned to Jeremy and Patsy. "This is your fault!" he hissed evilly. He just had time to press a button on a nearby console before a dozen aliens surrounded him and dragged him out of the control room. He was too busy kicking and screaming to say anything else.

"They don't mess about, this lot, do they?" whispered Patsy.

"That's what I'm afraid of," whispered Jeremy, watching Gruntox ordering buttons to be pushed and levers to be pulled.

The control room lights began to dim. Everything in the room seemed to blur and … slide? Gruntox spoke into a microphone on a flexible stalk, which he pulled out of the arm of his throne. His voice filled the entire area.

"This station will now melt down to its basic molecules! Recycling will then begin! Invasion force will withdraw and regroup! All staff and business partners to escape pods!

Everyone to escape pods!"

"What about us?" called Patsy.

"Humans will be ejected," growled Gruntox.

"Since we helped you out," said Jeremy quickly, "why not let us use the transporter door thing and go home?"

Gruntox thought for a moment. The ceiling was starting to drip and run down the walls, and the walls were starting to run across the floor.

"Very well," he grumbled reluctantly. "I am merciful."

With that, he hurried off towards the escape pods, followed closely by all the other aliens. The lights grew dimmer. Control consoles and display screens began to sag lazily.

"Better hurry," said Jeremy.

He placed a hand on the transporter portal's operating panel. The door slid back, but the vortex beyond it was dim and patchy, nothing like it had been before.

"No power!" cried Jeremy helplessly. "We won't get through! Or we might get through, but it'll dump us in space!" Then he remembered something. "Smith! That was what he did at the controls, before they dragged him away. The rotten sneak switched off the power!"

"So this is it," said Patsy. "We end up melted into nothing, millions of miles from home."

"Chin up, Patsy," said Jeremy, whose chin was pretty down at that moment. "There must be a way out of this. Did I ever tell you about the time I foiled a bank robbery with two walnuts and a bag of crisps?"

"Yes."

The control room continued to fold in on itself like a slowly deflating balloon. Machines were gradually melting together into pools of alien metals and plastics. One of the controls that had already dissolved into nothing was the one to turn the portal's power back on.

"What have we got?" mumbled Jeremy to himself. "What can we use?"

"Think of something!" shouted Patsy. "Before *all* the controls are gone!"

Jeremy tried to run over to the remaining consoles but found that his feet had sunk into the floor, which was rapidly turning into a sticky, squishy goo. "You'll have to operate it, Patsy! Quick, over there!"

"Operate what?" cried Patsy, jumping out of the way of a sudden floorslide. She dashed over to where Dungsit had been standing.

"There, next to you!" called Jeremy. "That screen shows a pile of school. Those must be the controls for that vacuum machine on Earth."

"So?"

"So drive it into the woods, and point it at the other transporter door thing! The suction might pull us clear from this end!"

Back on Earth, the scoopotron suddenly lurched backwards as Patsy yanked its control levers on Mars. It rose and fell in the air, and made noises like half a dozen cows trapped in a falling elevator. It spun, sending its long nozzle flapping wildly, before zooming off in a zigzag.

A battered and smoke-damaged huddle of teachers from Grotside School had collected on the edge of the woods. They spoke softly and calmly to each other, and took turns wiping mud off the Headmaster.

Here they were safe from exploding school buildings. What they weren't safe from was the scoopotron. It leaped into view over the trees, and with a flying twirl swatted them with its nozzle. They found themselves hurled into the air for the second time that day, but none of them could be bothered to scream this time.

"Haven't you got the hang of it yet, Patsy?"

"All right, all right, I'm doing my best!" Patsy pulled and pushed at the scoopotron's controls. "There! I think I've worked out how to dump the stuff that was already inside it!"

The scoopotron zigzagged into the woods, leaving the teachers to dig themselves free of the many tonnes of concrete that were now on top of them. It crashed into trees and vacuumed up squirrels.

Finally, the portal was in sight. Its door was open and the pale, powerless vortex stirred groggily beyond. The scoopotron swung around for a few moments, then settled into position about fifty metres away. Its nozzle snaked unsteadily in front of it.

"I see it!" called Patsy. "I can see the transporter thing!"

At that moment, the ceiling of the control room flopped sideways. A gaping hole opened up above them. Out through the hole swirled the control room's air. In through the hole swirled the red dust of the Martian plains.

"Now!" yelled Jeremy. "Switch the vacuum on!"

Patsy pulled a lever, which collapsed into mush in her hand. As the scoopotron started up on Earth, a powerful suction pulled at the portal in the woods, through the interplanetary vortex and into the control room. Jeremy's shoes were tugged free of the melted floor with a plop, and he shot into the vortex. Patsy, feeling the pull of the scoopotron, simply jumped up and let it yank her through.

The control room, and the rest of the aliens' base, shrank away into wobbly mounds of different coloured goo, which waited patiently for a recycling ship to pick them up.

Jeremy and Patsy whizzed through the vortex and out of the portal in the woods. They dug their fingers into the grass and held on tight to avoid being swallowed up by the scoopotron. The suction set their school uniforms flapping like washing hung out to dry in a hurricane. Their fingers slipped as the ground beneath them trembled.

But within moments, the force that was pulling at them subsided. Now that its controls on Mars had melted away, the scoopotron was beginning to drift. It rose and floated aimlessly above the trees. Its suction mechanism switched off, and the whine of its engines wound down.

The portal closed and locked itself. It bleeped twice, and then it too began to drift up above the trees. Both machines slowly moved off, and dwindled to weeny dots. And then they were gone.

Jeremy's voice broke the silence. "I think the aliens have recalled them to Mars."

Patsy sat up and smeared the grass from her hands down her blazer. "I'm starving," she said. "Now can we go to the chip shop?"

Pausing only for Jeremy to complain about how the melting floor had completely ruined his shoes, they set off to find Professor Killjoy and Dr Nicely (to tell them they'd need to find a new lab assistant), and not to the chip shop at all. They thought they'd avoid the school for the time being, since about a third of it was lying in ruins, and the teachers wouldn't be in the best of moods.

"When I write this up in my memoirs," said Jeremy, adjusting his tie, "I'll call the chapter 'How I Saved the Whole of the Earth From Certain Demolition'."

Patsy made a remark about Jeremy's memoirs that can't be repeated, but Jeremy wasn't listening. He could feel a sharp buzzing sensation in his completely ruined shoes.

Simon Cheshire has written stories since he was at school, but it was only after turning thirty that he realized "my mental age would never exceed ten and that, in children's books, I had finally found my natural habitat". *Jeremy Brown of the Secret Service* was Simon's first published book, followed closely by *Jeremy Brown and the Mummy's Curse* and *Jeremy Brown on Mars*. The stories, he claims, "are based entirely upon actual events. Only names, characters, plots, dialogue and descriptive content have been changed, to make them more believable." Simon is also the author of *They Melted His Brain!*, *Totally Unsuitable for Children*, *Me and My Big Mouse* and *Dirty Rotten Tricks*.

You can find out more about Simon Cheshire and his books by visiting his website, at http://uk.geocities.com/simoncheshireuk